E

ABERDEEN
CITY LIBRARIES
)v.uk/libraries

Return to . . . . .
or any other Aberdeen City Library
Please return/renew this item by the last day shown. Items may also be
renewed by phone or online

25TH NOV.
2007
J.F.

WITHDRAWN

Bender's Edge

A stranger rode into the town of Bender's Edge, a one-armed, hard-featured man seated on a coal-black stallion. The men of Wyoming's powerful Everett cow-outfit had tried to kill him five years before and had left him for dead beside the trail. But Wade Halleran had not died. Filled with savage determination to gain revenge on these men, he had fought back from death and had ridden the trail from the tall mountains and deserts of Nevada to this small cow town on the edge of the Everett range.

Unknown to him, word of his coming had raced ahead of him and the men of the Everett ranch under the unscrupulous Hugh Everett were waiting, determined that this time he would be dead before he had been twenty-four hours in Bender's Edge.

This blazing novel tells of a man's battle against great odds, of sudden death and six-gun action, and as well as his desperate search for his soul and self-respect.

Bender's Edge

Paul Marsden

A Black Horse Western

ROBERT HALE · LONDON

© 1966, 2003 John Glasby
First hardcover edition 2003
Originally published in paperback as
The Time of the Gunman by Chuck Adams

ISBN 0 7090 7295 3

Robert Hale Limited
Clerkenwell House
Clerkenwell Green
London EC1R 0HT

Typeset by
Derek Doyle & Associates, Liverpool.
Printed and bound in Great Britain by
Antony Rowe Limited, Wiltshire

CHAPTER ONE

Wyoming Trail

Wade Halleran rode into Bender's Edge from the north-west, with the storm following him in, with fork-tongued lightning crackling across the darkly-clouded heavens and the rain drifting in over the flat desert. He slowed his mount to a walk once he hit the main street of town, made a cigarette and lit it, sucking the smoke down into his lungs. It tasted raw and sharp on his palate as he drew it down and then let it out in slow pinches.

For more than twelve days he had ridden the Badlands of Wyoming, all the way out of the high ranges, leaving behind the shadows of the great hills that shimmered in the hazy heat, the flinty soil where only the bitter sage grew and the endless day heat rolled back in waves from the punished earth, forming a thin, half-seen turbulence around the trail. The smell in his nostrils had been only the dry, rendered-out scent of sun-baked earth and grass and the irritating yellow-red dust.

A tall, limber man with eyes half hidden under thick brows, he rode with a certain looseness about him that proclaimed him to be a rangeman and long exposure to the sun had burned his skin to a deep shade. He had

5

seen few other travellers on the trail he had ridden and these had been little more than tiny fragments of dust in the far distances. As a man used to riding the long trails alone, this had meant nothing to him; and for most of the time, his thoughts had been introspective and indrawn.

Now, the nature of the terrain had changed; not abruptly, but rather by slow degrees. There was broad grassland to the south of the town. He had noticed it in the distance shortly before the storm had swept in behind him, blotting out the westering sun. Good, lush pasture, he reflected. There was sure to be some big ranch there and it might well be that the man he had been searching for over a thousand miles of territory, was here. The trail had led him in this direction and although the scent had faded at times, there was now a deep conviction in him that his quarry was here.

He drew the last puff of smoke from the cigarette, flicked it away with his fingers. All those days on the trail wearied a man to the bone; maybe that was why he had been so glad to see the dark shape of the town looming close on the horizon; that and the chance of getting under cover before the storm broke about him. He had heard of the sudden late spring storms which blew up with very little warning. They could turn the dry, dusty roads through the cow-towns into quag-mires, rivers of muddy water within minutes.

Stabling his mount, he made his way along the boardwalk to the tall, two-storied building which stood head and shoulders above the other, the creaking, faded sign over the door proclaiming it to be The Trail's End Hotel. Slow-pacing through the lobby, he went over to the desk. A bath and then a good meal at the small restaurant down the road apiece from the hotel, with maybe a drink or two to wash away the trail dust from his parched throat and then a good night's sleep. These were the things he wanted at the moment, he told himself as he rested his hands flat on top of the desk. Clem Arnott could wait until tomorrow.

'What can I do for you, Mister?' inquired the clerk politely.

'I want a room for the night, and a bath first if you can fix it.'

'Sure,' nodded the other. He spun the book on the desk and handed Wade the pen, glanced at the name written there, but it was obvious from the look on his face that it meant nothing to him. 'I'll arrange for the swamper to haul the water for you, Mr Halleran. Should be ready in half an hour if that's all right.'

'That'll be fine,' Wade said. He took the key to his room, went up the narrow, gloomy staircase that creaked underfoot at every step, along the short corridor at the top to his room. It was small and sparsely furnished, but to a man who had been so long on the trail, it was good to sit in the chair by the window, completely relaxed, letting his lids fully down as he stretched his legs out straight in front of him.

He had not meant to go to sleep, but even the rumbling crash of thunder as the storm broke over the town did not wake him; he slept through it all, wakened only by a hand shaking his shoulder. It was the desk clerk, standing beside him. He said apologetically: 'I knocked several times on the door, Mr Halleran; but I reckon you must've been really tired. Your bath is ready whenever you want it.'

'Thanks.' He followed the other down the stairs and to the rear of the building, through a heavily-draperied opening and into the small room. The steam was rising in a misty cloud from the hot water and he lay and soaked the weariness and soreness from his limbs before redressing and going back into the lobby.

'I reckon I'll step outside for a bite to eat,' he told the clerk, handing in his key. 'I noticed a restaurant down the road apiece.'

The other nodded. 'I guessed you'd be wanting to eat, Mr Halleran. There was someone in askin' about you a little while ago. He said he'd be waiting for you in the saloon across the street as soon as you'd eaten.'

Wade drew his brows tightly together, forehead knit in surprised furrows. He shrugged. 'Did he say who he was?'

The clerk smiled. 'He didn't, Mr Halleran. But I know him. Reckon everybody in town knows Hugh Everett. Owns the biggest spread in these parts.' He lowered his tone confidentially, glanced about him for a moment, then went on quietly: 'Mr Everett is the law around Bender's Edge.' He spoke with a curiously exaggerated respect.

Wade gave a quick nod. 'Thanks,' he said curtly, his words harsher than he had intended. 'I reckon you've told me more than enough about him.'

Turning, he made his way out into the street. The storm that had followed him all that afternoon had almost passed. The sky to the north-west was clearing swiftly and the dark curtain of rain had moved on towards the grasslands to the south. It was almost dusk now, the sun hidden behind the clouds low on the horizon and the first sky sentinels were showing in the east. He kept to the boardwalk. The street was muddy, churned up by the horses' hoofs, and the wheels of wagons. Around him there was movement and talk. Most of the men he saw seemed to be headed for the saloons and as he expected, the restaurant was almost empty when he entered. He found a table away from the door, lowered himself into the chair and gave his order to the cook.

For the life of him he couldn't figure out why Hugh Everett should want to see him. Obviously the other had something on his mind. He decided not to trouble himself thinking about that until he had eaten. If Everett wanted to see him as urgently as that, then he would have to wait.

The food tasted good and for once it was well-cooked. He finished the meal with black coffee and a two-cent cigar, something he seldom did, smoking the cigar slowly, savouring the taste of the smoke on his palate. The restaurant had emptied while he had been eating and now there was only the cook, standing behind the bar, his weight resting cn his elbows. Wade saw the other's eyes drift speculatively in his direction.

Getting to his feet, he crossed over to the counter and laid a couple of coins in front of the other.

'Grub all right?' inquired the man.

'Best I've tasted in a long while.' Wade nodded. He turned to go for the door, then hesitated. Glancing back, he said disinterestedly, 'I noticed a big spread to the south of here when I rode in, figured I might get myself a job there. You know who owns the place?'

'That's the Everett spread you're talkin' about,' said the other, pocketing the coins. 'He pays well and they say he looks after the men who ride for him. Could be he's lookin' for more riders.'

'What sort of man is he? You know anythin' about him?'

The other shrugged. 'He's a rich man, maybe the richest between here and the border. Most of the men who ride for him are a tough bunch, gunslingers mainly.' As he spoke his gaze fell to the guns at Wade's waist, their butts worn smooth. 'You might get a job there if you try,' he went on tonelessly.

From the note in the other's voice, Wade gathered that the man thought little of Hugh Everett, but would not openly say so. He thought grimly to himself: If Everett was the real law in this part of the territory, then he might have ways of dealing with anybody who tried to speak out against him. Most men would keep their thoughts to themselves. Heading for the door, he turned over recent events in his mind. Maybe if Clem Arnott had ridden into Bender's Edge, he would have joined up with the Everett outfit, believing himself to be quite safe there. It was not going to be easy to prise him loose and if Arnott spotted him in town, it might bring the entire weight of the Everett crew down on his neck. These men would stick together thicker than flies if danger threatened one of them.

There were several men clustered around the entrance to the saloon which the hotel clerk had pointed out to him. They gave him bright-sharp stares as he went by them, more than curiosity showing on their faces. Reflected in the yellow lamplight from the saloon, their faces were etched with dark shadows. Wade watched them idly as he pushed open the swing doors and went inside the brightly-lit saloon.

It was not difficult to decide which of the men in the room was Hugh Everett. He sat at one of the tables, his back to the door, but there were several of his men behind him, watchfully alert, their hands never straying very far from their guns. Wade gave him a cursory glance, then walked across to the bar, laid his elbows on it and set his weight on them. The barkeep was a trifle slow in the way he brought the bottle and Wade noticed the oblique glance the other laid in the direction of the Everett boss. Placing the bottle and glass in front of him, the barkeep gave him a head-on glance.

'You new in town, mister?'

'That's right.'

'Just ridin' through, or you got somethin' in mind?' There was suspicion in every line of the other's sagging features, in the set of his jawline. Wade stared him out. He had met this type before, men wanting to be big, having a puffed-up idea of their own importance. Maybe he felt secure in whatever he was trying to prove, knowing that Hugh Everett was there, with most of his men. Wade said thinly: 'You ask far too many questions, friend.'

The barkeep started up, stepping back a pace, hands

stretched out in front of him, the fingers straight and rigid. His eyes flared with a sudden anger, but a glance at the guns strapped to Wade's wrist made him pause and keep that anger well under control.

Wade went on tautly: 'You usually question men who ride into this town?'

'Rein up a little, mister,' said a voice behind Wade. He turned to find that Everett had thrown down his cards on to the table in front of him and risen quietly to his feet. The rancher came forward, stood beside Wade, leaning against the bar. Out of the corner of his mouth, he said to the barkeep, 'All right, Joe, beat it!'

'Yes, sir, Mister Everett.' The bartender moved off and busied himself with a wet rag at the far end of the bar, wiping up the stains.

'You're sure doggoned touchy,' the grey-haired man said. He laid a cool, appraising glance on the younger man's face. 'Folk just like to know who they have here. This is still a frontier town, very much so, and we've had our share of desperadoes ridin' in and shootin' the place up.'

Wade shrugged, said nothing. He reached out for his glass and drained it in a single gulp. The raw liquor burned the back of his throat, but it washed away the taste of alkali and brought a fresh sense of warmth to the pit of his stomach.

'Have one on me.' Everett nodded towards the bottle, waited until Wade had filled the glass, then said quietly: 'You're probably wonderin' who I am and why I'm interested in you.'

Wade was briefly silent, then a hint of hard irony appeared around the edges of his mouth. 'I already know who you are, Mister Everett. They tell me you own the biggest cattle spread in these parts. What I don't know is why you left that message with the hotel clerk that you wanted to see me, that you'd be waitin' here in the saloon for me to come over.'

'Well now, I'll come straight to the point. I saw you ride into town late this afternoon and I reckon I know a good rangeman when I see one. I particularly liked the look of that horse you were ridin' – a good cow-pony and I don't doubt that you know how to handle those guns you're wearin'.'

'I've done my share of riding,' Wade said tightly. 'But it could be that I'm not in town lookin' for a job.'

Everett raised his brows a little. There was a thoughtful look on his face and the smile which had been there only a few moments before suddenly atrophied. He straightened up a little at this reply. 'Maybe I have you figured wrong, my friend,' he murmured after a short, reflective pause. 'It could be that you're here in town lookin' for trouble. I feel I ought to warn you that the law is not too kindly disposed towards men who come to make trouble. We've had our share in the past and we want no more.'

'But of course, you're the law here in Bender's Edge, aren't you, Mister Everett,' Wade said softly.

The other snapped harshly – 'I like to see that things are done right. But whoever told you that I made the law here was lyin'. We have a Sheriff in town and it's his duty to see that law and order are kept.' The other tilted the whiskey bottle, slopped the amber liquid into a clean glass, tossed it down quickly, grimacing a little as he did so. Without turning, he said: 'You see the men in this saloon, they all work for me, every one of 'em. And this is only part of my crew. There are twice as many on the rangeland now, tendin' to the herd. I pay good money for men who work for me. Forty dollars a month and all found. If I were you, I'd think it over carefully if you mean to stay in town for any length of time.'

'I'll think about it,' Wade said. Deliberately he turned back to the counter, poured a drink and sipped it slowly, staring into the crystal mirror that ran the full length of the wall at the back of the bar. In it, he saw Everett staring tautly at him, the other's lips compressed into a thin, hard line. The rancher was trying to keep a tight rein on his temper. Evidently this was a situation he had not met before. Usually, whenever anyone drifted into town, he was only too pleased to jump at the chance of riding for the Everett crew, particularly for pay such as this, which Wade knew was almost twenty dollars more than the usual rates of pay for a working cowhand. It could be, too, that most of the drifters coming here were men with a price on their heads, staying one jump ahead of the law, with the smell of gunsmoke still clinging to them, and he did not doubt that Everett was a sufficiently powerful man to be able to protect the men who worked for him, even against the law.

Finally, Everett said: 'You just think it over, Halleran. I wouldn't want you to make a mistake. This can be a funny sort of town to strangers. Accidents have been known to happen in the streets, especially after dark.' The way he said it, the words were so obviously a threat that Wade gave no indication that he had heard them.

Wade emptied his glass, set it down on the counter. His grin widened. Turning, he fixed a long look at the other, 'Not a very hospitable kind of place, is it?'

Everett shrugged. 'It is for those we like,' he said carelessly. He seemed to have swallowed his earlier anger. 'But don't take too long in makin' up your mind about this job. It won't stay open for you indefinitely.' A pause, then he continued: 'You know, I've got a feelin' about you, Halleran.' His sharp eyes lingered on Wade's face, as though he were trying to remember something from the past. There was probably a file in the man's mind, Wade thought to himself, with a faint feeling of amusement, and he was trying to riffle through the wanted notices he had seen, looking for his face on one of them.

'What sort of feelin' is it, Everett?'

For a moment, judging from the expression in his eyes, there was something balanced in the older man's mind. Then he seemed to thrust it away with an effort, said shortly: 'Nothin'. Like I told you, we don't get many strangers here in town.'

He turned on his heel, moved back to the table. The small knot of men parted to let him through, then took up their places behind him as he sat down to play, picking up the cards and going on with the game he had interrupted some minutes before. Casually, Wade let his sharp-eyed gaze wander over the men clustered around the tables, or along the bar, looking for a face that might be familiar, the face of the man he had ridden close on three hundred miles to find; the man who had shot down an unarmed man in a gambling saloon and then lit out west as fast as his bronc would carry him, knowing that sooner or later there would be a deadly retribution following close on his heels. But there was nobody there who faintly resembled Arnott and finishing his drink, he made his way to the door, pushed it open with the flat of his hand and walked out into the cool night. The storm of the afternoon had cleared the air, had washed all of the clinging dust out of the sky, so that the stars shone with an unusual brilliance in their yeasty ferment where they sprawled across the great inverted bowl of the night sky. Down on the eastern horizon, just lifting clear of the far rim of the world, a round moon was shining yellowly as it climbed slowly, almost ponderously up into the heavens.

The wind that sighed along the main street was cold and fresh, still moist from the rains. He pulled the high collar of his mackinaw jacket higher about his neck as he stepped off the boardwalk into the street, angled over to the hotel. As he walked he thought about Hugh Everett. There was a lot about the man that he did not

14

like, that had inwardly riled him from the first moment of their meeting. His arrogance, his ruthless confidence in himself and his belief that he could have any man he wanted on his payroll, either because of the money he was prepared to pay, or because of the threat of trouble he could instil into them. His thoughts were abruptly scattered by the sound of gunshots from the far edge of town, followed almost at once by the thunder of riders heading along the main street. He lengthened his stride to get to the other side, saw the slim figure that had stepped off the boardwalk and was making its way towards him.

A voice, loud and anonymous shouted something in the distance and silhouetted against the shafts of light that spilled into the street from the buildings some fifty yards away, he saw the three riders bearing down on them, urging their horses forward at a swift gallop, firing their pistols into the air. The sound of the oncoming horses was dull and heavy in the drying mud of the street, seemed suddenly to grow out of all proportion and he saw that the girl, her head jerking round at the sound, would be directly in their path. With a cry of warning, he ran forward, caught her around the waist, and hurried her back to the boardwalk, helping her up as the men thundered towards the saloon. His hand was on the butt of his gun when the girl said sharply: 'This is no concern of yours. Stay out of it!'

'But they deliberately tried to run you down,' he said tautly.

'Keep your gun holstered.' There was an urgent insistence in her tone. 'Please. Do as I say.'

Relaxing his hold on her waist, he allowed his other arm to drop limply to his side, the gun still in leather. The girl nodded her head, and he thought, although he was not sure, that he heard a faint sigh come from her lips. She drew herself up to her full height, and her head was so close to his shoulder that he could smell the scent of her hair, could see her features, calm and composed, and her lips drew back from her teeth in a faint smile.

'Had you drawn your gun you would have had the whole of the Everett crew down on you. Then we might both have been killed.'

'I might have guessed they were more of that bunch,' he said bitterly. He stared across the street as the three men dropped from their saddles, still on the run, looped the reins over the hitching rail, holstered their six-guns and moved towards the saloon. Stepping up on to the boardwalk, their features were plainly shown in the blaze of yellow light that spilled over the door in front of them and it was in that yellow instant, that he saw the face of the man he was looking for, saw it clearly and without any possibility of a mistake. It looked a little older than when he had known it before and there seemed to be a few more lines on it, but it was Clem Arnott all right. Probably here, though, he thought, the other might go under a different name. Just in case there was trouble close behind him.

Wade's fingers caught around the girl's arm, biting in with a steel-like strength. He said harshly: 'That man there, just going into the saloon. Do you know him?'

The girl looked across the street, then nodded. For a moment there was a look of mild surprise on her face. Then she said quietly: 'I know him.'

'Who is he?'

'Why that's Clem Everett. Hugh Everett's nephew. He got back here about four weeks ago.'

'Clem Everett.' Wade smiled without mirth. It was something he had not expected and it meant that he might have to revise any plans he may have made for taking his revenge on the other for the slaying of his brother. He had intended to ride into town, check on the other, then maybe call him out, face him in the

16

street and shoot him down. That had been the one burning thought uppermost in his mind all these long, vengeance-filled days. But if he killed Hugh Everett's nephew, his chances of riding out of Bender's Edge again were very slim. He could, however, imagine how safe the other felt now. He was back on his own stamping grounds, his uncle was the most powerful man in this part of the territory and he would feel sure in his belief that nobody could touch him now, whatever he had done.

Back in his room at the hotel, Wade lay on the low bed, his hands clasped at the back of his neck, and tried to think things out in the light of what he now knew. It would be no use going to the Sheriff and seeking the support of the law. The chances were that the Sheriff would immediately pass on to Hugh Everett anything that Wade told him and his stay in town would be very brief indeed before they carried him out and gave him a pemanent resting place up in the cemetery.

He gave his thoughts a prolonged study, turning over ideas in his mind and rejecting the majority of them outright. In the morning, he told himself, he would ride out and take a look around the perimeter of the Everett spread. The chances were that it would stretch for many miles in every direction and if Clem did make a trip out to the more remote parts, then it might provide him with the chance he needed to force a showdown.

As he crossed a low ridge and rode down towards the creek that shone with a bright glitter a quarter of a mile away, Wade's horse increased its gait of its own accord. The sun had lifted almost to its zenith and the blast of heat had been a heavy, oppressive thing, pressing and enveloping him, sucking all of the moisture in him to the surface. Here, on the eastern edge of the Everett spread, the ground was rough and inhospitable. It was evident from what he had seen that morning, that Hugh Everett had grabbed off all of the best grazing land for himself, either by staking out at the very beginning, or forcing the small ranchers to sell out to him. Judging from what he had seen of the other the previous evening, Wade did not doubt that Everett would have his own ways of seeing to it that these smaller men sold out at only a fraction of what their land was worth. It needed only a couple of bad summers in succession to bring a man virtually to his knees, to force him to seek money from somewhere to keep going, in the hope that the third year would be good and more than make up for the other two; and if, as he suspected, Everett also owned the bank in Bender's Edge, he would hold the mortgage on the ranches. When the note fell due and there was no chance of being paid, he would simply take over the place and so, over the years his spread would have grown at the expense of the others. It all fitted in with the crew he needed to ensure that there was no trouble. Anyone who tried to stand against him would be trampled down. The old ways of greed and violence, never-changing, never different, wherever one rode along this great western frontier.

Letting his mount drink, giving it a chance to blow, he dismounted, walked to the lip of the rise and stared about him. Here, the grassland had given way to eroded ground, copper-coloured by the sand that shifted into a multitude of shapes and chasms, whenever the wind caught it and whirled it ahead of it. Turning, he looked across the creek at the dense curtain of vegetation that covered the brush country. In the distance it hazed out into open desert, a trackless waste that stretched for the best part of fifty miles or more to the south. Here, nearer at hand, a mass of chaparral and mesquite thickets interspersed with patches of prickly pear and Spanish dagger made riding a tricky and painful business, but it was the only way to go.

Stepping back into the saddle, wiping the sweat from his forehead, he rubbed the spot where the sweatband of his hat had cut into his skin, chafing it into an itching sore, then pulled the brim down over his eyes to keep out as much of the sunglare as possible. The brush country that formed the boundary here for the Everett ranch, was a long, secretive belt of ground that ran between two high ridges that cut off all sight of the rolling grassland to the north. It was a place of dried-out creek beds and harsh, weathered rocks; a bristling, sombre mass which he did not like the look of. His mount shied away from the clumps of Spanish dagger and he was forced to touch its flanks with the rowels of his spurs to inch it forward.

A swarm of biting brown flies came up out of nowhere and settled on his face and exposed skin, and halfway into the vegetation he reined up his mount and shaded his eyes with his hand, trying to make out the lie of the land around him, not wanting to go too deep until it was absolutely necessary. Any open wounds caused by the spearlike leaves of the Spanish dagger would be fed upon by the swarms of these brittle brown flies, goading the horse into a frenzy of pain.

With no knowledge at all where the Everett outfit might be, he turned back, continued his slow circle of the ranch. Here and there he spotted the fence which was the perimeter of the spread and once, during the late part of the afternoon, he made out the darkly moving shadow of cattle on the hills in the distance, but they were too far away for him to see if they were tended by men from the cattle crew and the ground was far too open for him to dare to ride through the perimeter fence and take a closer look.

As he rode, he told himself that he was doing this

19

the hard way. If he wanted to get Clem Everett he stood a far better chance in town. Get somebody to fetch the other out of the saloon on some pretext and call him out in the street. But that idea too, presented its difficulties. He might get his chance of meeting the other on even terms, but he would still have to go against the whole weight of the Everett crew, who would inevitably accompany the other into town.

Shortly before nightfall he had fully circled the southern edge of the spread, was riding through pine which grew on a long, low ridge overlooking the prairie. A wealth of dark shadows lay below him and at the end of a sharp, quick rise, he found himself looking down on to a camp fire that stood out starkly against the dark background. The silhouettes of riders showed briefly against the red glow of the flames. There was an instant of quiet. An instant in which Wade Halleran drew a deep breath into his lungs and leaned forward in the saddle.

That did not look like a line camp down there. There was no herd nearby, yet he figured there were probably half a dozen men down there, making camp for the night. Wade's gaze moved over the clearing and a moment later he made out the wide trail that led up on to the ridge, meeting it perhaps three hundred yards from where he sat. On the other side of the ridge he had seen the small ranch, set in its own boundary fence, a spread belonging to one of the other ranchers in the area adjoining the Everett spread.

Better step down, he thought; and keep a watch on the men down there. He felt a vague stirring of suspicion in his mind. Nothing definite, just the feeling that those men were not down there to watch any of Everett's cattle, more to bring other steers into the Everett fold. There had been some talk in town of rustling among the small herds in the territory around Bender's Edge. Once or twice he had heard Everett's name mentioned in connection with the rustling. Nobody would dare to speak out aloud against the rancher, that much was for sure. Everett would have a quick and permanent way of making sure that he did not spread such talk again.

Now that it was after sundown, the air held a cool nip to it and stepping down from the saddle he moved his mount further back into the trees, squatted on the lip of the ridge where he could keep a close watch on the men around the camp fire, and ate a little of the jerked beef he had brought with him, tearing it into strips with his strong teeth and chewing on it for some time, letting his digestive juices work on it before allowing it to slide down his throat. He washed it down with cold water from a nearby stream.

Sitting there, he rolled himself a smoke, hunched his shoulders as he lit it and watched the world around him plunge into the deeper darkness of night. A little breeze had sprung up, freshening now, stirring the leaves on the trees above him and beyond them, in the utter velvet blackness of the heavens, the stars came out, sprinkled across the yeasty ferment of the universe. The moon had not yet risen, but he knew it would soon come up, full and round, and give the men down below plenty of light by which to see.

He smoked his cigarette slowly, turning things over in his mind. If Hugh Everett was getting cattle by raiding the herds of the smaller ranchers, then it would be at places such as this that he would send his men across the boundary wires, to single out a couple of hundred head maybe, and drive them back on to the Everett range. Once there, it would be a relatively simple matter for these men to alter the brands and if the other ranchers tried to make any protest, any charge against him, they were bound to fail. He knew now why the other was the law in Bender's Edge and the surrounding territory. There was no one big enough in these parts to stand against him.

Stretching himself out on his blanket, he settled down to await events. When he heard the distant run of a horse off to the north-east, he lifted himself up from his blankets, got to his knees and peered down on to the plain below. Someone had thrust a fresh bundle of kindling on to the fire, for it suddenly blazed brilliantly in a shower of sparks that lifted and were then caught by the breeze and whirled away in a stream of crimson.

Wade listened to the horse come on, the steady tattoo of its hoofs on the earth sounding louder with every passing minute, and he felt a blend of interest and caution rising in him.

For a moment, in the dimness, he could see nothing, although there was a faint yellow glow in the east where the moon was just below the horizon, throwing a pale light over the terrain. The men around the fire were clearly visible now, standing in an expectant group, looking towards the oncoming rider. A few moments later he materialized out of the darkness and even at that distance, even in the dimness, Wade recognized him at once. He felt the cool wash of anger go through him, felt his fingers curl, the nails digging into the palms of his hands.

Clem Arnott, alias Clem Everett. His brother's murderer. The man who would gun down an unarmed man and then head out of town and ride for the security of his own spread. Grimly, Wade wondered if old Hugh Everett knew what his nephew had done, the sort of ruthless killer he was. Somehow, he doubted it, although he felt certain that if he did, he would continue to protect him, even against the law.

Well he, Wade Halleran was not the law. He knew only the law of the six-gun and that of an eye for an eye, and a tooth for a tooth. He had started out by watching the men with suspicion. Now there was something else to it.

He made up his blanket roll in quick time, lashed it to the saddle. He had the feeling that the men down there would soon be on the move now that the boss's nephew had arrived to give the orders. At the moment he was not sure what he would do, but it might be possible, in the inevitable confusion which would attend the rustling of cattle over the ridge. that he might get an even chance at Clem Everett without the rest of the men having a chance to interfere.

CHAPTER TWO

Halleran Hits Out

It was half-an-hour later when the men kicked out the fire, moved to their horses and saddled up. By now the moon was up, huge and yellow in the east, throwing its cold, clear light over the terrain, picking out the crevasses and the large boulders with streaks of midnight shadow. Wade watched them closely as they put their mounts to the steep upgrade that led towards the crest of the ridge. The trail made a solid streak of dust that glowed silver among the shadows and it was easy for him to follow the progress of the tight knot of men as they moved through the moonlight. The group of riders pushed hard against the hills as they cut up from the plain.

He let them get to the top of the ridge before kicking his own mount along the flanks with his heels, moving forward among the trees. The horse frequently slowed, knowing its own mind, and he had to keep urging it on. Dust stayed with him all the way over the razor-backed ridge and down the other side and the stillness had the tag-ends of sound in it, noises that were not quite faded out, giving him the impression of more than one group of riders criss-crossing down into the dimness in their urgent hastes. Half-an-hour brought him to the gaping mouth of a canyon. It lay athwart the trail, its rocky floor filled by a slash of black shadow thrown by the moon. He reined up and eyed it apprehensively for a long moment. He had no way of telling how far it progressed into the rocks and he had no wish to be trapped in there by the riders when they came back, driving their stolen cattle ahead of them. Even as he sat there, taut and temporarily undecided in the saddle, he caught the break of gunfire in the distance, little flutters of sound carried down to him by the wind. They came from higher away than the trail on which he was and from the fact that there were only a few, seemingly disconnected shots, he guessed that the rustlers of the Everett crew were driving the cattle along the trail, back over the hills. It was possible that they had also run into trouble and had been forced to fight it out with the other cattle crew, but he did not doubt that they had been doing this for a sufficiently long period now to be able to take care of themselves.

He drew back from the canyon, moved off into the shadows thrown by the rocks to one side, waited with a growing sense of impatience which he tried hard to fight and control. Ten minutes later he heard the firing die away, fading into the stillness which seemed more pronounced by virtue of the racket that had gone before. After that he heard the thunder of oncoming hoofs. He lifted his head and looked anxiously at the shadowed bank on either side of the trail where it narrowed prior to running into the steep-sided canyon. The column was dead ahead, moving into the canyon at the far end. He heard the change in the sound of their hoofs, shoved his horse flat against the bank nearby. He was almost completely absorbed by the dark shadows thrown by the moon.

Slackening speed as it moved through the steep-sided canyon, the lowing herd raced through, urged on by the men bringing up the rear. Wade estimated that there were close on three hundred head in the column: a good haul for a single night's work. It was small wonder that Hugh Everett had grown to be such a rich and powerful man in so short a time.

The steers surged forward, bellowing as they thundered through the gap and out into the open. The dust drag hung in the air, getting into Wade's nostrils, irritating his eyes.

Boxed against the steep wall of rock, tufted here and there with coarse vegetation, Wade watched through narrowed eyes. Two men burst into the open, standing in their stirrups, stiff-legged, yelling harshly at the tops of their voices. Choking the narrow exit, the confused river of steers and riders swayed through in one relentless motion. The men in view rode back and forth restlessly, keeping the steers well bunched as they herded them along to the trail that wound out of sight over the ridge. More men broke cover. Wade eyed them closely. One of the men reined up as the last of the drag came through. He waved an arm to the others and as he lifted himself in the saddle, the moonlight fell full on his features and he saw it was Clem Everett. His hand reached down and touched the smooth butt of the Colt at his waist. Almost, he pulled it clear of leather. Why not shoot the other down now, from cover? He could kill Everett without trouble at this almost point-blank range and be up in the hills before the rest of the men with him knew what had happened. By that time they would have little chance of trailing him, not with this milling herd on their hands, ready to run in stampede if a gun exploded in their ears.

With an effort he put the idea out of his mind. He wanted Everett to know who killed him and why. In that split second before the other died, he had to know who had pulled the trigger which sent him into eternity. The herd raced on over the ridge, streaming down the far side. Five of the men rode after it. Now there was only Everett and one other man, moving towards the ridge, a little away from the trail. Wade could wait no longer. Gently, he eased his mount forward so that he was now clear of the shadow. At first Everett did not see him. The other was staring back into the dark chasm of the canyon, as if expecting trouble to come riding close on their heels.

Then Everett turned in the saddle, lifted the reins, ready to urge his mount forward after the steers, as though satisfied that there was no immediate danger from behind. He saw Wade's horse standing still, motionless, and at once he froze in the saddle. Peering forward, he said harshly: 'That you, Charley?'

'No,' said Wade tautly. Out of the corner of his eye he saw that the other crew member was near the top of the ridge, had neither noticed nor heard anything. 'You know who I am, Everett. It's been a long time since you shot down my brother in cold blood. You knew he was unarmed and in those days you called yourself Arnott. Maybe you figured you'd be safe once you got back here.'

There was a slow, but perceptible stiffening of the other's body from the knees to the shoulders. He turned his head very slowly to look after the other man, his tongue flicking out to lick his dry lips. 'You've got the wrong man, mister,' he said, trying to force confidence into his voice. 'And if you know what's good for you, you'll turn that horse of yours and ride out of here.'

26

Wade shook his head very slowly, his lips drawn back into a grim, tight smile. 'Easy won't do it now, Everett. There's blood on your hands and I mean to wipe it clean now. I'm givin' you an even chance, which is more than a murderin' snake such as you deserves. Now go for your gun and quit stallin'.'

Still there was no move on the other's part. Wade guessed that he was trying to delay any showdown until one of his men realized that he had not rejoined them and rode back to see what had happened.

'You won't shoot me down in cold blood, mister,' said the other thinly. 'And if I don't intend to draw against you, if I just turn my horse and ride on out of here, you'd have to shoot me in the back, and I figure you ain't the type of man to do that. You got some kind of code of honour that says a man has to face you with a gun in his hand before you kill him.'

'Don't stake your life on that, Everett. Maybe you'd be right in most cases, but not with a snake who shoots an unarmed man down.' Wade's voice had gone softly quiet, so that it carried no further than the other. Going on, he said: 'Everett, don't think you can drag this out until one of your men comes a-lookin' for you. I'm goin' to count up to five and then draw. It's up to you if you want to defend yourself.'

'Count if you like, it won't make any difference.' Everett knew that he needed an edge against this man. Shooting down that unarmed cowboy who had beaten him at poker had been child's play. He had known that the other did not pack a gun when he had sat in the game with him. Now he knew that this tall, self-assured gunman who sat just beyond the shadows in front of him, was far faster than he was. He tried a ruse that almost worked. Scarcely had he finished speaking than he jerked on the reins of his mount as if to carry out his threat and ride out, leaving Wade to shoot him in the back if he dared. But a second later, still turning, he stiffened abruptly, his right shoulder went down and he struck for his gun, his taloned fingers blurring down for the holster at his side.

Twin muzzle-blasts exploded almost together. Echoes ran tumultuously from the explosions, rattled off the high walls of the canyon and blurred together into a single atrophying echo at the far end. For a moment, Everett sat high in the saddle, his right hand hanging by his side, a look of stunned surprise written on his features. Then his facial muscles slackened, his jaw dropped open and he toppled forward, sliding sideways out of the saddle, hitting the ground with a hollow sound. His mount jerked at the movement, reared up, then swung about, startled.

For a moment Wade remained where he was, staring down at the humped body of the dead man lying among the rocks. The riderless horse raced along the trail and over the ridge. It would not be long before the rest of that Everett crew came high-tailing it back to find out what had happened. Hauling swiftly on the reins, he rode up towards the higher ground on the side of the trail. A shot echoed from behind him and he felt the wind of the bullet fanning his cheek as it scorched past him and whined off the rocks in a shrill ricochet. Throwing a swift glance over his shoulder, he saw that two of the men had ridden back over the ridge, were spurring their mounts after him. Neither paused to take a look at Clem Everett, lying face downward in the rocks. It was as if they knew instinctively that he was dead, beyond their aid, and their main concern now was to capture, or at least identify, the other's killer. Now old Hugh Everett would not rest until he had caught his nephew's murderer. Whatever the other had done to deserve this, would count as nothing as far as the old man was concerned.

Slamming a quick succession of bullets along the narrow trail, he urged his mount up the steeply-angled trail which was just visible in the flooding moonlight.

'There he goes!' yelled one of the men harshly. Another shot punctuated his words.

In one of those brief flashes of reasoning that a man experiences in a crisis such as this, Wade estimated that his headlong start would give him at best, only a couple of hundred yards advantage of the two men on his trail. He felt that if he could maintain this until he reached the top of the high wall of rock, his mount would outrun the others once they were down the far slope and out on to more level ground. His horse was tired. He could feel that in the way he sometimes slipped, staggered and almost fell headlong back down the slope, the loose shale shifting treacherously underfoot. But it was of thoroughbred stock, used to this, and he did not doubt that it would stay ahead of its pursuers. He pushed it to the limit, clinging tightly to the reins with his hand, while he thrust fresh shells into the empty chambers of his gun. His head was low over the bronc's neck to present a more difficult target. Rowelling his spurs into the animal's flanks, he forced it on, up the slope, around a huge boulder that barred his way at the top and out on to more level ground. The lip of the ridge where it extended high above the canyon, was flatter and wider than he had thought. A couple of slugs hammered leadenly against the boulder as he rode around it. Down below he heard one of the men yell a sudden order to the other and a moment later picked up the sound of a horse moving alongside his trail, but below him. Somebody was trying to cut him off, he thought grimly. Savagely, he pulled the horse's head round, rode diagonally across the top of the ridge, hit the downgrade slope and went down it in a series of bounding leaps. Several times the horse almost went down on to its nose and he could do nothing to help it beyond sitting straight-legged in the saddle. But each time it managed to right itself with a convulsive heave and continue on. They hit the mesa at the bottom of the slope, ran forward into dark shadow. Behind him he caught a fragmentary glimpse of the two horsemen coming out on to the skyline, staring down into the darkness of the valley. In the distance there was a frenzied lowing of the rustled herd. Reining up, Wade watched the men, ready to take off again if they made a move to head down the slope after him, but after a few moments they wheeled their mounts sharply and vanished from sight. They would take the rustled cattle in, while some of them would take Clem's body back to the ranch house and break the news to his uncle. Eyes stabbing ahead into the moon-shadowed dimness, he rode swiftly over the mesa. Here and there the ground was studded with gopher holes that could not be seen until one was on top of them. If he slowed his mount to a walk there was the danger that he might run into more of Everett's men, so he had no choice but to continue at this headlong speed and trust to his luck. Somehow he made it to the far edge of the mesa, riding past the tall, sky-rearing buttes that lifted themselves up from the plain like great buildings of stone, gleaming palely in the moonlight.

Cutting over the low ridge that marked the northern boundary of the mesa, he deliberately rode his mount over stone, leaving a trail which not even an Apache could have followed. Threading his way along the narrow, descending bed of a ravine, he came out into the valley that ran alongside the Everett range to the west, moved around gigantic boulders that almost blocked the trail at this point and came out into the open ground that stretched from left to right across his gaze. Nothing moved in the white moonlight and in the distance, perhaps three miles away, he saw the thick club of trees, well off any trail and headed towards them. He wasn't exactly sure what he was going to do now. He had expected to experience a feeling of deep satisfaction now that he had finished what he had set out to do, now that he had avenged his brother's cold-blooded murder. But curiously, there was nothing like that. Certainly Clem Everett was not the first man he had killed in fair fight, but now he sensed only a strange feeling of emptiness in his mind, a curious hollowness which he did not like.

He was tempted to ride out to the west and keep on riding, find whichever trail he could and follow it to the end: then maybe he would find another and someday reach a spot where he could stay and let the smell of gun-smoke wear off.

But there was the feeling that this was maybe what the rannies back there would expect him to do and they knew this country far better than he did. His safest place could well be in Bender's Edge. It was possibly the last place where Hugh Everett would think of looking for him. Inwardly, he did not doubt that both of those men who had followed him up the ridge had recognized him, would be able to give a description of him to Everett which the rancher would recognize at once. A stranger rode into town, deliberately refused the offer to work for the biggest spread in the territory, was absent from town the night that Clem Everett was killed. It did not need a blind man to see that there was, in all probability, some connection between these events.

After thirty minutes' slow travel over the range, he came to the trees, moved deeply into them to a spot where he could not be seen, and built himself a fire. Here, deep in the brush, the red glow would not be visible anywhere outside the trees and he fried himself up a little of the jerky, not hungry, but chewing on it reflectively before washing it down with water from his canteen, and smoking one last cigarette before he put down his blankets and stretched out under them.

Presently he was asleep.

*

A sharp-edged stone, grinding in the small of his back, woke Wade when it was still dark. The moon had drifted over the sky and was now lowering in the west, still bright enough to show him the silhouettes of the trees. His fire had burned out, was now mostly ash with only a faint red glow in its heart. As he lay there he debated whether to get up and put fresh kindling on to it, then sat up sharply as his mount whinnied softly from the brush nearby.

There was the feel of danger about him in the utter stillness. It was too quiet. Then, from far below him, somewhere out on the plain, he heard the first faint murmur of men riding hard. Standing up, he moved out to the fringe of the trees, crouched down, and pushed his sight out into the moonlit dimness. The utter quiet was a signal of the things to come and he felt the tiny hairs on the nape of his neck riffle as he hunched himself forward. The riders were pushing their horses at a cruel, punishing pace and the sound of their hoofs was a steady abrasion in the night, growing louder and nearer.

He spotted them about ten minutes later, cutting slantwise across the mesa in the direction of the trees. Scouring wind sighed through the trees, cooling the sweat that had started out on his body. There was no doubting who those men were, nor why they were here. The band who had rustled that bunch of steers had evidently wasted no time in riding hell for leather back to the ranch and informing Hugh Everett of what had happened. And old Hugh had wasted no time in getting a bunch of his men together and riding out on his trail. How they had come on him so soon, he did not know. But the precariousness of his position was forced on him as he saw the incoming men fan out at a signal from the man in the lead.

There was no time in which to saddle up and ride out. Long before he managed to do that they would have swung round the knoll and cut off any hope of retreat from the position.

The riders heading directly for him paused less than fifty yards from the outer fringe of trees, so close that he was able to recognize Hugh Everett and the two men who had pursued him after he had shot down the old man's nephew.

'He's in there someplace,' roared Everett. 'There's a fifty dollar bonus to the man who brings him out, dead or alive.'

'What makes you so damned sure he's in there?' called one of the other men out on the edge of the line. 'He could've headed for the border durin' the night.'

'Those tracks back there led in this direction,' countered Everett. 'I say he had to rest up someplace and he couldn't be anywhere else but here. It's the only cover for miles around. Now get in there after him.'

Slowly Wade drew the guns from their holsters, pulled himself up on his knees on the thick carpet of pine needles. He listened to the faint sound of the riders as they worked their way around the knoll. The men halted when they were still some distance away. To attempt to come back on horseback into the trees would be fatal, for there was no way of moving through the thickly tangled undergrowth to the spot where he was hidden, without making sufficient noise to be seen at once.

Kicking earth over the embers of the fire, he edged back into the brush. His dilemma now was that he could not watch all sides at once and he suspected that the riders would attempt to rush him when they moved in. All of them were now alert to his presence there.

From the endless quiet of the trees, he tracked the movement of one group, moving in from the south. Everett, he knew, would remain out of range, leaving the dirty work to his men. He judged that the men moving in from the north would not be in position yet. They had to move around the knoll and approach slowly and cautiously from the rear.

He stood up now, easing himself forward. Then he got to thinking how he might turn this situation to his own advantage. These two groups of men were edging towards each other in the darkness, trigger-happy men who would fire at shadows, who would shoot first and ask questions later. Ducking swiftly into the brush, he caught his mount, led it a little off to the right. Behind him he was able to pick out the sound of men moving cautiously through the tight undergrowth on his trail. They would take their time, he reasoned, not wanting to walk into an ambush, knowing him for a deadly killer, a fast man with a gun. Even a hardened gunman did not go up against another unless he was sure of his ground.

He twisted once, to look back into the dark, deep shadows, saw a man move through the outer fringe of trees, perhaps thirty yards away, hesitate, and then duck into the brush. Another came close on his heels, darting forward, shadow blending with the overall blarkness of the forest.

Wade held to the shadows, keeping a tight hold on his mount, praying that it would make no whinneying sound to give warning of his position. He paused frequently to listen, knowing that it would not be long before the two groups of men met. If, as he figured, they were both taut-nerved and trigger-happy, they might start firing at each other before they discovered their mistake. This was what he was banking on: that and the possibility of reaching the far edge of the trees and riding on out in the ensuing confusion. From the moon-washed clearing that opened out to his left, he clearly heard the soft crush of booted feet moving through the angle-high grass, moving around into the trees which cut off his view in that direction. He glided briefly across a patch of moonlight, expecting to hear the sound of a shout or a shot that would mean he had been seen, then shifted back into shadow again, and still no sound from his left. There was a brief hurrying sound of a man very close and he held his hand over his mount's muzzle as he crouched down, every muscle and nerve poised in his body as the man moved among the bushes. Stone-like, he strained his eyes, watching for a shifting silhouette, knowing that if the other spotted him, he would be forced to drop the other and make a break for it. A murky shape formed up in the gloom. The man was moving with difficulty, trying to push his way through the entangling branches without making a sound. Wade's horse lifted its head sharply as it sensed the presence of the man out there. With an effort, he tightened his grip on it, held his breath until it hurt in his lungs.

There came the solid sound of something heavy striking the trunk of one of the trees, followed by a softly muttered curse. The man hesitated then went on and a few moments later, passed from Wade's sight. Letting his breath go through his nostrils, Wade moved forward. That man had passed a little too close for his liking. Stopping a little while later, he stared about him, studying his terrain. The trees thinned a few yards ahead of him, opening out on to a canyon that made a slow turn into darker country. The left-hand wall of the canyon remained sheer for as far as he could see it and as he moved his glance slowly over the scene, he made out the shapes of the horses, clustered in a tight group halfway along the canyon. If he could spook the horses it would reduce the chances of him being caught.

He stepped out of the trees, still leading his mount. Behind him there came a sudden shout, clearly echoing among the trees. A split second later and a gunshot sounded, muffled by the thick brush, but unmistakable. A man gave up a great cry in the stillness that followed; then there came confused shouting. In the distance he heard Hugh Everett's bull-like roar sounding above the babble of voices, demanding to know what was going on among the trees.

'Right, horse,' he said to his mount as he pulled the cinch tight, then swung up into the saddle, thrusting the six-gun back into its holster as he kicked at his horse's flanks. Everett was still shouting and it would not take long for the men in there to realize that somehow he had slipped through their fingers in the dark underbrush. Presently this canyon would be riddled like a sieve with bullets. He was twenty feet from the trees, riding down into the dark V of the canyon when a man shouted from the trees at his back. 'There he goes, goddamnit! He's gettin' away.'

A volley crashed out, cracking through the trees, the bullets whining off the rocks on either side. The distance was almost two hundred yards now, too far for anything but aimed rifle fire to be accurate and he knew that most of the gunfire was falling short. He reined up as he reached the horses, leaned from the saddle and loosened the tie ropes, fired a couple of shots into the air, sent their mounts plunging along the dark canyon. They would not stop until they were several miles away, too far for men to round them up on foot.

He ran his horse along the canyon, came out into the open half a mile further along. Across the rough shoulders of a ridge he saw that the sweeping country beyond was almost perfectly flat, glistening a little in the pale, cold light of the full moon. Everett had been right when he had said that there was no other place but among those trees where a man could hide.

Total silence closed down, except for the drumming of his own mount. A mile further on he came to the wide river that ran across the trail. The rains of the past few days had brought it up and the current was in flood. Here and there, in the strongly swirling waters, he caught sight of large logs, carried down from the hills where the river was born, jetting huge columns of white-foamed water high into the air as the logs struck the submerged rocks in their onward rush. He cast about him for any spot where it might be easier and safer to ford the river than at this point, but could see none. Far off to his right it swept round a bend and it was easy to see, even from that distance, where the swift, powerful current had gouged fresh earth from the banks, eroding them at several points.

It would waste precious time to ride along the river's edge to try to find some other point to cross. Not only that, but it would be easy for the men at his back to follow his tracks in the soft soil that bordered the bank. He let his breath sound in a long sigh. There was nothing for it but to put his horse across here although the animal was tired. The sight of a dust cloud behind him forced the issue. Everett had wasted no time in bringing the rest of his men after him. He reckoned that in less than a quarter of an hour they would be at the river.

He had no choice now. Pointing the horse upstream for a better footing on the river bed, he felt the current break against the animal's chest and lungs; and he was nowhere near the half-way point. He kept his eyes on the river now, watching where the moonlight splashed silver on the rushing water, knowing that at the speed the current was racing, he would have very little warning of danger. It needed only one of those logs to smash into them and both horse and rider would be finished, if not killed outright, then drowned long before they managed to fight their way back to the bank.

There were also the rocks to be watched. Here the danger was more insidious and treacherous. For the most part they were submerged beneath the water, just making their presence known by the faint streak of foam that formed where the current broke above them.

Sand churned up under the horse's feet brought bubbles to the surface. A short distance and the bottom dropped suddenly away. Wade remained in the saddle for a few moments, then slid out of it, clinging to the reins, easing the burden on the horse as it swam for the far bank, letting the current carry it a little way. Near the middle of the river the horse's legs struck ground, and a moment later Wade felt his feet jar on the sandbar. His mount hauled him forward on to his face and he lay there for several moments, spitting the muddy water from his mouth, sucking air down into his lungs.

'Easy there, boy.' he said hoarsely 'We'll get our wind back here and then go the rest of the way.'

As if it understood his words, the horse stood absolutely still, a little more sure of itself now that it was on relatively solid ground. Wade threw a swift glance over his shoulder, across the racing torrent. He could see nothing of his pursuers now and for a moment the thought occurred to him that perhaps they had lost his trail in the dimness. Then he saw them climb a low rise less than a mile away, knew they were still on his trail.

Cold closed like a misty blanket around him and he felt the icy chill in his legs where his soaked clothing hung about his flesh, chafing with every move he made. There was no time to pause now. Any moment and he would be in full view of those riders. Catching the reins, he moved to the edge of the sandbar, contemplated the swiftly-swirling waters for a further moment, then plunged in, the horse slipping into the river beside him. There was no way of telling how deep the river was between the sandbar and the far bank but within half a minute they were drifting downstream with the current, fighting for the other bank that moved past them at an almost frightening speed. Wade knew better than to try and struggle. So long as he was able to keep his head above water and his hold on the reins, he had a chance. Once he lost his head and threshed wildly in the water, he would go under, dragged down by the vicious flow. A tree trunk surged past him, the rough bark scraping his leg as it passed. He saw it go tumbling end over end as it struck a hidden rock. The warning signal came almost too late. Struggling desperately with the reins, he hauled on them with all of his strength, bringing the horse's head round, guiding it to one side. Whirled downstream, they scraped past the submerged rock with scant inches to spare. Then they had reached a steep bend in the river and now the current was fighting with them, swinging them in to the bank.

Three minutes later, three hard minutes during which the river, as if loth to give them up, tumbled horse and rider into each other as the rocky bed, close to the bank, scratched and tore at them. With all of the breath battered from his bruised and half-senseless body, Wade knelt there in the shallow water at the river's edge, resting his weight on his hands and knees, head hanging down between his arms as the water ran off him and his chest heaved with every single gasping breath he took, as he tried to draw air down into his heaving lungs.

Staggering to his feet, he moved towards the horse that stood patiently in the long grass which here grew right down to the very edge of the river.

Floundering through the ankle-deep water, he reached the horse and pulled himself up into the saddle with a painful wrench of arm and shoulder muscles. His body was bitterly cold and his teeth were chattering in his head as he wheeled the bay away from the bank and headed out over the grasslands.

Above him, the pale moon looked down, round and cold and utterly remote. In the outer darkness, somewhere off among the hills, a coyote howled a mournful dirge at the heavens, a weird, hacking cry that sent a fresh shiver along his veins.

Wade's mouth was a thin, hard line as he rode swiftly across the moonlit plain. It would not take long for the riders at his back to cross that river and head out after him, and if they had managed to pick up his trail among those rocks above the trail where he had out-gunned Clem Everett, they would surely be able to follow tracks in the soft, muddy ground near the river. Normally, he reckoned, a man would pause and think twice about crossing that river in full flood and at night, but with Hugh Everett forcing his men on, thinking of nothing but vengeance, there would be no holding them. Keyed to an alert tautness he watched the nature of the terrain change slowly as he rode. Very soon there were dense thickets of mesquite and chaparral and sword-grass that struck viciously at the horse's legs, making it shy away every time they came near it. This was not ordinary brush country. He did not know how far it stretched, but he recognized that he would be caught if he tried to ride around the fringe where there was only cactus and prickly pear. A score of yards further in and it became a veritable jungle, dry and harsh, with the leaves and stalks cracking under the hoofs of his mount.

In the dead and oppressive silence, he rode as fast as he dared, wondering if the men pursuing him would be thrown off the scent when they reached here, whether they would take him for a man not fool enough to try to head through it. As he moved further into the savage, harsh brushland, he kept a look out for small and narrow game trails which would save his mount from the slashing vegetation. In places the ground began to rise, became more rocky, but still not as open as he would have liked. His horse too, had become nervous. It's feet were sore and bleeding from the attentions of the cutting, sword-like leaves that slashed it from every side and at length he was forced to halt it, to soothe it as best he could. It stood absolutely still, ears flattened, shivering violently.

He waited for five minutes for it to calm down, lifted himself then high in the saddle, peering about him in the fading light of the setting moon, striving to see how much further this inhospitable country extended, whether there was any sign at all that he was heading out of it. Perhaps two miles away, there was a low ridge of red sandstone that lifted itself clear of the plain, standing out starkly against the flatter terrain around it. A game trail was just visible, cutting away from him to one side and he judged that it probably led to the ridge. It seemed as good a trail as any to follow and he was on the point of gigging his mount forward when he picked out the sound of riders, a sound that came and grew in the silence. They were, from the direction of the sounds, heading in from the direction of the river and he sucked in a gust of air as he swivelled his head and managed to just make them out, a tightly-packed punch of men, half-obscured by the dust kicked up by their horses.

He knew instinctively that if Hugh Everett reckoned he was in this country, he would not hesitate to ride in through the thickest part of the vegetation to get at him. It would be typical of the man to think he would do things the hard way and he would guess that Wade had elected to ride through this godforsaken spot as the quickest way of getting out of the area.

But he would not rush into it headlong. It was the sort of terrain which a man would hesitate to comb for a killer; for apart from the snakes and lizards which abounded there, not to mention the vegetation itself, it was ideal country from which a man could fire from ambush.

With an effort he kept a tight hold on himself, his ears and eyes taking in everything there was to hear and see. When he was satisfied that the men with Everett were keeping together this time, that they had entered the thickets and were working their way towards him, he turned and moved his mount out slowly, resisting the urge to spur it to speed, knowing that in the dry vegetation any swift movement would kick up such a racket that those men would instantly hear it and guess at his position. He managed to pick out the swish and crack of branches as they moved through the low, stunted trees on the fringe of the scrubland; and after a little while, the muted murmur of voices as they came closer.

Now was the time for concealment and a mountain man's craft, he reflected, not for speed and blind flight from these men. Cutting along the game trail he found that it soon moved upgrade, rising steeply, then levelling off in the form of a small plateau. It was as he was riding across one of those isolated patches of level ground that he heard a man's shout behind him. It was followed by the sharp whiplash of a rifle shot. The bullet struck wide of Wade's position, but he knew that he had been seen in the dim moonlight. From somewhere off to his right there was a fainter, answering shout.

There was no time to waste now. Wade raced along the game track, swung around a bend and saw to his consternation that it narrowed and finally vanished into a tunnel through a thick wall of mesquite. Low trees faced him and he realized that he would somehow have to ride his mount through them if he was to get clear and reach the high ridge which dominated the plain.

Lowering his head, clinging tightly to the reins, he ran the horse through the narrow tunnel. Snake-like branches whipped at his head and shoulders as they plunged through. The sharp-pointed leaves stabbed his legs and thorns tore his flesh like a multitude of dagger thrusts. He almost fell from the saddle as a branch struck him high on the shoulder sending a vicious stab of pain along his right arm. For a moment he was out of sight of the men pursuing him, but a fusillade of slugs tore into the greenery after him, searching him out. He could hear them whipping and droning through the brush on either side of him.

Almost blinded by the thin branches that struck his face and across his eyes, he gritted his teeth, was acutely aware that there was blood trickling down the side of his face from a dozen deep gouges. Behind him, the guns were still blasting and there were shouts of men closing in rapidly. He could make only slow progress here. His clothes were torn and shredded and beneath them his skin was ripped and it was only with an effort that he managed to keep a tight rein on his nerves and keep moving. His mount wanted to stop, to try to turn back and it was all he could do to make it go on. There was not much sound now that the firing had stopped, but even the silence that hung like a thick curtain all about him, was ominous, shrieking soundlessly in his ears. He could visualize the men circling the brush, moving in on him from all sides. The slight sounds that he did pick up told him that the men were on foot, working their way carefully in after him. This time they would not let him slip through their fingers as he had before.

God, how much further did this damned brush go? He wiped at his face, smearing the blood all over his cheeks and on to the backs of his hands. The men behind him would comb every possible inch of ground in the vicinity.

Most of the sound seemed to be a little to the right and behind him, and it decided his direction. Without thinking almost, he swung the horse off the narrow trail, headed it into denser brush. It was a mistake. He realized this before he had gone a couple of yards, but by then it was too late for him to turn back. He had committed himself and was now forced to go on. Soon it became obvious that the men were working to a set pattern as they closed in on him, hemming him in from all sides. He twisted his head round as the horse, maddened by the slashing thorns and branches, plunged forward, tried to make out the shapes of the men on his heels. He could see nothing, turned his head and saw, too late, the thick overhead branches which clustered above the narrow trail, directly in front of him. There was no time in which he could do anything. He half threw up one arm to shield his face, then felt the lowermost branch, as thick and unyielding as a man's arm, strike him a stunning blow over the forehead.

The impact knocked him out of the saddle, sent him sprawling into the thick brush. He hit the ground hard, lay for several moments, struggling to keep a grip on his buckling consciousness. Somewhere close at hand, he could hear the crash of men pushing their way through the undergrowth. Dimly, he heard a man shout something harshly at the top of his voice. A second later he spotted the other, stepping out from the dark shadows a few feet away, his gun levelled on Wade's prone body.

With an effort Wade forced his mind to clear a little. Jerking his body to one side, he whipped out his Colt as he did so, sighted the weapon, cocked and thumbed back the hammer, letting it fall on the cartridge in the chamber. The slug hit the man high in the chest, jerking him back on his feet, so that he seemed to be literally standing on tiptoe, his shoulders thrown back, spine arched in a curious fashion. For an incredible moment the other remained on his feet, teetering as he struggled to hold life in his body, to lift the gun in his hand and bring the barrel to bear on Wade's body. Wade fired again as the other, with the last ounce of strength in his body, squeezed the trigger. The slug caught Wade on the side of the head, burning along his skull just above the ear.

A dense blackness threatened to overwhelm him. Dimly, as though in a dream, he was aware of other guns firing now as the men closed in on him, realized that he had fallen into a trap of his own making. His left arm burned as a slug tore through flesh and muscle into the bone. He felt another and then there was nothing as the blackness engulfed him completely.

Slowly, cautiously, the four men pushed their way through the thorn and mesquite, guns drawn, barrels levelled at the man who lay face-downward in the underbrush. One of them stepped close, turned Wade Halleran's body over with the toe of his boot, gave a brief nod to the others.

'Dead,' he said shortly. 'I guess that's the end of the trail for this murderin' killer.'

One of the other men rubbed the back of his hand over his forehead, where a thorny strand, whipping without warning from the darkness, had brought blood from his flesh. 'Let's get back to Everett and give him the news,' he said hoarsely. 'The sooner I'm out of this godforsaken place the better I'll like it.'

Turning, they retraced their steps, picking their way carefully through the dense brush. This was the haunt of hammerheads and cottonmouths and the bite of either could prove fatal.

Hugh Everett sat taut in the saddle, fingers gripping the reins with white-knuckled hold. His face was fixed and still as he said: 'Where's Halleran?'

'Back there a spell,' said the tallest of the four men. 'You got no call to worry any more, boss. He's dead.'

Everett let a faint sigh go from him. His face remained hard and utterly cold. Without another word, he wheeled his mount, rode down through the chaparral and mesquite to where the dawn was just beginning to brighten the eastern sky.

CHAPTER THREE

Trail Out

But Wade Halleran was not dead; and death did not come. Several times during the night his mind surged up from the dark depths of unconsciousness, broke the surface of reality, only to sink back again as the weakness swept through his body, the blood pulsing from his wounds. When he finally did come round, there was a pulsed roaring in his ears like a vast and thunderous waterfall inside his skull. His lungs seemed to be starved of air and all he could do for several minutes was lie there on the damp ground, gasping harshly for breath, the green vegetation around him advancing and receding in front of his twisting vision. He felt curiously light-headed and there was a constricting band around his chest, growing tighter with every passing second.

With an effort that taxed the last ounce of strength in his weakened body, he forced himself over on to his side, propping himself up on his right elbow. There was no feeling now in his left arm. The wounds had stopped bleeding, the blood congealed during the cold hours before the dawn. Pain gripped him in sharp, fiery hands and every movement he made, however slight, sent stabs of agony lancing through him.

He was utterly limp now but deep in his mind there was the knowledge that if he was to live, he would have to get out of this tangled wilderness, into the open and, if possible, find his mount. There was no sign of the men who had been pursuing him and he figured they believed him dead. They would have ridden back to the Everett ranch by now. In spite of this he would not be safe until he was out of the territory. In his present state he would make an excellent target for any gunman who happened along. Sucking air down into his lungs, he forced himself to his knees. His left arm was useless. Glancing down at it he saw the sodden rags that covered it, knew he had lost a lot of blood, that there were probably several pieces of lead still embedded in it near the bone. Groping his way forward, trying to see through his pain-blurred vision, he moved to the east. The sun was up now, although he could not see it for the thick, tangled branches over his head, but there was a growing heat in the air that told him it had been above the horizon for some hours, although he had little way of telling how long he had lain there in the undergrowth like a dead man.

It was a painful, almost impossible task. Only a man such as Wade Halleran would have stuck it out. He crawled for some yards, then stopped. At times, utterly exhausted by his efforts, he collapsed on to his face and was forced to remain there, unable to move until he had gathered his strength once more. It was almost noon as far as he was able to judge, when he finally crawled out of the chaparral, out of the shade of the low, stunted trees and into open country. The rearing bluffs were now less than a quarter of a mile away, glowing redly in the harsh sunglare. On two occasions his wounds had opened again, had begun bleeding, and a swarm of brittle brown flies had attacked him, settling on the open sores in their dozens. The pain almost drove him insane and there was very little he could do to prevent them from settling on him, with one arm useless and the other necessary to drag himself forward over the rough, uneven ground.

There was no sign of his mount. Whether it had made off when the shooting had started close by, or whether the men from the Everett crew had caught it and taken it with them, he did not know. He pondered the idea heavily, but got no satisfaction out of it and put the thought from his mind. Now that he was out of the brush he tried to get to his feet. After several unsuccessful attempts, he succeeded, staggered a little, swaying as the blood rushed, thumping painfully to his forehead. Gingerly he put up his right hand to his skull, winced as his fingers touched the long crease in his skull. An inch the other way and that bullet would have killed him. He tightened his lips, forced himself to think clearly. As it was, his chances of survival were very slender.

He walked stumblingly over the glaring whiteness of the ground, heading in the direction of the bluffs. He had no idea what he would do once he got there, but it was the only landmark for miles around and as such, he made for it. The sun reached its zenith, the heat-head reached its piled-up intensity, enveloping every-thing, the baked earth, the rocks that reflected the heat and glare in sickening, dizzying waves, the very air itself that seemed to have been drawn over some vast inferno before it reached him. For most of the time he staggered forward with no idea of where he was, moving in a delirium, muttering incoherent words under his breath, eyes narrowed to mere slits in a vain attempt to keep out the all-pervading glare. Waves of nausea threatened to overwhelm him, churning his stomach painfully. He retched drily, knew there was no water to be had in this parched and terrible land.

There were few shadows on the ground when he

Item(s) Borrowed

Branch: Tillydrone Library
Date: 26/10/2020   **Time:** 10:15 AM
ID: 63356000718387

ITEM(S)   DUE DATE

Bender's Edge   23 Nov 2020
X000000283699

The bounty man   23 Nov 2020
X000000295356

Your current loan(s): 4
Your current reservation(s): 0
Your current active request(s): 0

Please retain this receipt and return items on or before
the due date

finally reached the bluffs and because of the altitude of
the sun, these were necessarily short. But somehow he
managed to crawl into shade and here he fell into a
semi-conscious doze; his mind swamped by the ener-
vating weakness which had now become an integral
part of him. His throat was dry and parched, lips
swollen to twice their normal size and it was painfully
difficult to swallow. During the long, heat-filled afternoon, with the sun a blazing, eye-searing disc in the
brassy, cloudless heavens, a wind started up, blowing
the dry alkaline dust off the desert against the bluffs.
After a while he managed to pull himself together,
crawl around the rearing, sandstone walls until he
found a narrow crack which went back into the stone a
little way and here he pushed himself, struggling to get
as far as possible out of the way of the stinging,
maddening grains of dust that swirled about him in an
orange-red cloud. It was as if nature herself were
determined to conspire against him.

His clouded mind sank into the abysmal darkness of
unconsciousness again, enveloping him in a merciful
blackness. There were long shadows over the ground
when he woke once more, with grudging consciousness
returning in a feeling of numbed pain. He tried to move
his legs, winced as pain laced through his muscles, but
by forcing himself to ignore it, he succeeded in working
his way out of the crack in the sandstone bluff. The
wind had died and with the sun low on the western
horizon, touching everything with a blood-red glow,
there was a welcome clearness and a coolness in the
air.

Standing, legs rubber-like under him, steadying
himself with his good arm against the smooth rock, he
stood for several minutes, drawing the clean, pure air
down into his aching lungs, feeling a little of his
strength returning to his bruised and battered body.
His left arm throbbed a little now and he knew that he

49

would have to get medical aid soon. He had heard of
men who had died from poisoning because of lead in
their bodies.

Thrusting one leg in front of the other, he moved
away from the bluffs, down the slope and out towards
the flat, featureless face of the desert. He continued
to move east, scarcely conscious of why he did so,
only knowing that he had to move continually in one
direction, otherwise he would wander around in
circles in this terrible wilderness until he died of
thirst or from his wounds.

There was little of his jacket and shirt left. The clawing thorny branches back there in the thickets had
seen to that and as the darkness fell, the chill air
caught at his body, adding its own discomfort. But at
least it kept him awake, acting in the same manner as
a splash of cold water on his face. He kept a tight hold
on himself as he moved forward through the night,
steering himself by the moon when it finally rose, a
little after full, giving him plenty of light to see by.
Once he thought he heard the drumming of hoofs in
the distance, but it was difficult to distinguish between
this and the throbbing of blood through his temples.

He saw nothing and guessed it was the blood pounding
in his head or a figment of his overwrought imagination.
Minutes ticked themselves by into a soundless, pain-filled
eternity. It must have been around midnight when he
intersected a narrow trail that wound like a silver thread
into the shadow-darkened plain. He cut along it, came to
a wide clearing around which grew virgin birch, jutting
out of the huge boulders that lay in a tumbled confusion
around the trail.

Near the top of the trail, where it wound between
two tall boulders, he stopped abruptly. From behind one
of the rocks protruded a horse's rump, the tail twitching
a little. The thought occurred to him that this was just
another illusion brought on by his delirium. Sliding his

gun from leather, he edged his way cautiously forward.
The shock of seeing the animal had brought a clearness
to his mind and he was acutely aware of his own
danger. His gaze probing at the surrounding brush, he
moved around the side of the rock, slid a little to one
side, lifted his head carefully an inch at a time. From
his vantage point he was able to make out the horse
clearly. It stood patiently, hipshot, not tethered as he
would have expected it to be if someone had left it there
while he had gone off scouting the brush. The horse was
saddled and bridled however. Moving down the slope
towards the base of the rocks, he came up to the animal.
It shied away from him as he approached, then paused,
trembling a little as he murmured soothingly to it,
patted its neck. Why had its rider left it here? he
wondered. Evidently he had gone off hurriedly, for there
were no hobbles. It was as if he intended to return, yet
from the manner in which the horse stood, he reckoned
it had been there for some time.

Puzzled, he moved off a few yards, scouting the edge
of the clearing. Not until he reached the point further
from the horse, did he find the answer to the riddle. The
sprawled body of the man lay wedged between two
boulders, lying face-downward. Bending, Wade examined the body. The man had been shot in the back and
there were at least two slugs in him. He had died without having the chance to draw his gun from leather.
Thrusting his own weapon back into its holster, Wade
straightened, gritting his teeth as pain lanced through
him.

Several minutes passed before he guessed what had
happened. This was evidently one of the men who had
been guarding that other herd when Clem Everett and
his men had ridden up to rustle it. The other had been
shot down without a chance to defend himself and for
some strange reason his mount had refused to leave
the spot.

51

But what had been this man's misfortune had been Wade's gain. With an effort that cost him much, he hauled himself one-handed into the saddle. As though it realized he was badly hurt, the horse stood patiently while he settled himself, then started forward once he touched it with the spurs, winding its way down through the rocks. The slender birches lifted high on either side of them and there was a stray breeze funnelling along the trail that soothed the burning agony of his face and head.

Shortly before dawn, he reached a wider trail, swung to the north and by the time the first pale streaks of grey were showing in the east he was within sight of a small town, dark and silent yet. The danger of going into the village, still being so close to the Everett spread, outweighed the desire to find a doctor for his wounds. He swung around the cluster of buildings, skirted the place to the north, then narrowed his eyes as he saw something he had not expected, something that gave him new hope.

There was a railhead to the north of the village and a train of boxcars standing in the marshalling yards. Reining up on top of a low rise, he watched the scene closely. The locomotive had been connected to the cars and already had steam up. There were a few men working around the locomotive, but all of the boxcars seemed to have been prepared and there was nobody near them. This was the chance to get out of this territory. He knew that it would not be long before he collapsed from sheer weakness and exhaustion, that he had to get into one of those cars before the train pulled out. Keeping well to the lee of the rise, he rode down the slope as far as he dared. He could hear the shouts of the men in the distance, listened to them with only a part of his mind. He felt horribly weak as he swung out of the saddle, almost fell, putting out his arm against the warm flanks of the horse. Sobbing for breath he slithered down the steep slope towards the gleaming rails, stumbled over them towards the cars, keeping them between him and the men. Moving along the train, he found one with the door not fully closed and sealed.

Straining with all of his remaining strength, he managed to force the door open, to haul himself over the lip of the opening and on to the cold, wooden floor inside. He lay there for several seconds, summoning up the rest of his strength to turn, get to his feet and pull the door shut. There was pitch blackness inside the car and he was forced to feel his way forward until he reached one corner, where he sank down on to his back and lay unable to move, until a little of the feeling seeped back into his body. There was the faint murmur of voices outside the car, a mutter of conversation as the men paused momentarily just outside the door. A feeling of panic swept through him. Supposing they noticed that the door hadn't been sealed and rectified that mistake? How would he get out again without being found?

Gradually, the fear subsided as the men moved away. Settling his shoulders against the side of the boxcar, he closed his eyes and surrendered himself reluctantly to the weakness and lassitude that overwhelmed him. When he woke, an unfathomable time later, it was to feel the car moving and swaying under him, to hear the monotonous click of the wheels on the rails. For a moment, he debated whether to get up, to try to see where they were, but he decided against this. Although his stomach was protesting with hunger and his throat was parched with thirst, he knew that he needed rest. Accordingly, he sank back, closed his eyes and slept again.

How long he slept he did not know. When he opened his eyes again and looked about him, he saw that the darkness inside the car was not as absolute as it had been before, that he could make out the outlines of several large barrels in the far corner where the light shone in through chinks in the walls. He guessed it was late morning or early afternoon. The heat inside the boxcar was stifling and sweat lay on his body as he tried to think things out clearly. He had little idea of which direction the train was taking him. East probably, although it might have swung north. Wherever it was, at least it would have taken him away from Bender's Edge. He did not think that Hugh Everett would have men watching for him now and it was unlikely that he would send men back for his body.

Getting to his feet, he moved over to the door, gripped the handle tightly in his good hand and pulled with all of his strength. It opened slowly, sliding along its runners and he peered out, blinking in the strong sunlight which glared harshly at him. Trees moved by swiftly in a blur of green shadow and glancing back he could make out the gleaming track as it stretched away into the distance, round a wide curve. The train was moving quickly, seemed to be picking up speed and the rush of air congealed the sweat on his body.

Judging by the position of the sun he reckoned it was around two o'clock in the afternoon, which meant that they had been travelling for the best part of six hours. By now he could be two or three hundred miles from Bender's Edge – and trouble.

The sun lowered slowly, giving him an indication of direction and he guessed they were moving north-east. Going back into the boxcar, he sank down on to the swaying floor and examined his wounds. It was the first time since he had been left for dead that he had had the opportunity to do this. The wound along the side of his skull was a deep gash, and he had lost a lot of blood from it, but the slug had glanced off the bone and he reckoned there was little actual damage done there. But his left arm had at least three slugs embed-

ded in it and it seemed swollen, an ugly purplish colour
around the ragged edges of the wounds. Blood had
caked the skin and his entire arm ached and throbbed
dully every time he tried to move it.

He lay in a kind of stupor for several hours. The
sunlight outside began to fade and presently he heard
the locomotive utter a loud, piercing wail, felt the slackening in the speed of the train. They were probably
nearing their destination he thought fiercely; and it was
essential that he should get out before they ran into the
railyards and the vanmen came along and discovered
him. If they did that, there might be a lot of awkward
questions to answer and in his present condition he had
little desire to answer them. Besides, if word once got
back to Hugh Everett he did not doubt that the rancher
would get his men to testify that it had not been a fair
fight, but that he had deliberately ambushed Clem
Everett and shot him down in cold blood; and when it
came to a showdown, a jury would believe a man like
Everett in preference to himself.

He realized then that it would not be difficult for
Everett to build up a case of murder against him that
would stick. Scrambling to his feet he went back to the
door of the car, thrust it aside, glanced out. The sun
was almost on the rim of the undulating black mass of
hills in the near distance and shadows were long and
huge on the ground all about the track. A quick look in
the direction of the locomotive and he was able to make
out the dark smear of shadow in the distance which
marked the town towards which they were headed.
Another few minutes and they would be pulling into
the railyard. At the moment they were running
through a narrow valley, with tall trees on either side
and a smooth embankment which ran alongside the
track. A few thorn bushes grew out of the ground which
seemed, in places, to be soft and marshy and judging
the best spot, gritting his teeth, he plunged from the

slowing train. The ground came up to meet him in a rush and a blur of green, he hit hard, was unable to prevent the shriek of pain from passing his lips as he struck and rolled over several times, until he came to rest at the bottom of the slope.

How long he lay there fighting for consciousness, it was impossible for him to tell. When his mind finally cleared, he lay for a time peering up at the dark purple patch of sky, just visible through a gap in the branches over his head. Then he twisted his head sideways, saw the trunk of a tree rearing up from the marshy ground a couple of feet away, knew that luck had held for him once again.

With an effort, he thrust away to his feet, stood looking about him for a long moment, his brain clearing rapidly. He was some distance from the railroad and the trees in front of him stretched for some distance, running up along a ridge that overlooked the town. He moved into the trees cautiously, found a track and followed it. Eventually it led him out on to a broader, solid-beaten trail less than two hundred yards from the outskirts of the town. A few yellow lights showed in some of the windows, but for the most part this side of town seemed empty and deserted. He judged that it contained the stores and warehouses, a busy place during the daytime, but deserted at night, once the storekeepers had locked up their premises and moved into town. There was the open stretch of ground to be crossed, but it was almost dark and he decided to risk it. He had to find out where he was and get to a doctor as soon as possible. Then he needed food and drink.

Moving carefully through the dark alleys, he located the doctor's surgery fifteen minutes later. There was still a faint glow of yellow lamplight in the window and when he rapped loudly on the door there was only a momentary pause before he picked out the shuffle of footsteps approaching. The door opened and a white-haired man stood peering at him in the dimness.

'Are you the doctor?' Wade asked thickly. He had difficulty in standing. Everything seemed to be swimming around him and the other's face kept blurring and receding from him in a confusing manner.'

'That's right. I'm Doc Banner. But—'

'I need help.' Wade got out. He tried to say something more, but his knees buckled under him and he slumped forward, would have fallen on his face had not the other reached out and caught him.

There was a long period when Wade Halleran knew very little of what went on around him. Brief periods of relative rationality when he knew there was someone in the room with him, were interspersed by longer periods of unconsciousness or delirium. But there eventually came a day when he woke with his mind clear, aware of the hunger in his stomach.

With an effort, he turned his head and looked about him. There was nothing familiar in the room in which he lay. He could not recall having seen it before. While he was staring about him the door opened and a man came into the room, closing the door gently behind him, moved over to the bed. There was a faint smile on his face.

'How are you feelin' now?' asked the other. 'You've been fevered for a long time now. I was beginnin' to despair of you ever comin' out of it.'

Wade licked his lips. He felt strange, yet it was something he could not place. There was a soreness in his left shoulder and then he remembered the bullet wounds, that long hard journey to this town. He turned his head very slowly, tried to fight down the shock of horror that went through him. There was a look of utter disbelief on his face as he turned back to the other, tried to push himself up on to his right arm.

Gently, the grey-haired man thrust him back on to the pillow. He tried to fight him for a moment, then relaxed weakly. 'My arm,' he said through shaking lips. 'What happened to my arm?'

'I'm sorry, son,' said the other, his voice very low. 'I did everythin' I could to save it, but the poison from that lead and from some infection you got into those wounds had spread too far, there was nothing else I could do. If I hadn't amputated, you'd have been dead by now and—'

'Then for God's sake why didn't you let me die?'

The other shook his head. 'I couldn't do that, son,' he said reprovingly. 'I'm a doctor. Besides, it was obvious to me that you'd come a long way to get here in spite of your wounds and the blood you'd lost. Seemed to me you had somethin' on your mind, somethin' you had to do. I reckoned if it was as important as that, then it was up to me to save your life, even if I had to take drastic measures to do it.'

'But of what use is a one-armed man?' The bitterness in Wade's voice was something he could not hold back. Gradually the anger in him built up, anger against those men of the Everett cattle crew who had hunted him down and shot him as he lay unconscious; anger against Hugh Everett, the man who had given the orders, and anger against Clem Everett, who had started this chain of events when he had shot down Wade's brother.

'I know how you must be feelin' now, son,' said the other. He placed his fingers on Wade's wrist, feeling for the pulse. 'But believe me, you'll feel different in a little while. And if you ever want to tell me about it any time, I'll be here ready to listen'.

Wade was silent for a long moment, knew that the other was watching him closely with an expectant look in his eyes, head cocked a little to one side. 'It doesn't make a very pretty story,' he said finally. 'I don't want to talk about it right now. I've got a hell of a lot of thinkin' to do.'

'Sure, sure.' The other released his hold on his wrist, placed his hand on the blankets. 'I guess you'll be hungry now. I'll get somethin for you to eat. Then maybe you'll feel better.'

When he had gone Wade lay on his back, staring up at the ceiling over his head, but seeing nothing. It was difficult for him to control the feelings in his mind at that particular moment. The loss of his arm was only just beginning to seep into his numbed mind. He felt only half a man and at the moment he reckoned that any ideas he may have had of riding back to Bender's Edge and gaining his revenge over Hugh Everett and his riders, was doomed. What chance would a one-armed gunman have against that crew of hired killers?

Sucking in a sharp breath he rubbed his forehead with the back of his hand, felt the cold sweat on his flesh. There was still a weakness in his body, but he knew instinctively that the other had patched him up well. Apart from the loss of his arm, he was almost as good as new.

The doctor came back a few minutes later with a bowl of hot stew and some bread He sat them down on a tray in front of Wade, propping him up on the pillows. While he ate, the other watched him from beneath lowered lids, evidently wanting to ask questions, but not sure how to go about it. Finally, he said: 'It's obvious to me that you were in a gunfight someplace. What happened? An ambush on the trail?'

'Not exactly.' Wade shook his head, spooned the hot stew into his mouth, chewing on it slowly. 'Just where is this place?'

For a moment there was a look of surprise on the other's face, an expression quickly gone. 'Selina,' he said quietly 'You mean you didn't know where you were when you came to me?'

'I'd been hitchin' a ride on a train,' Wade said harshly. He held out the cup and waited until the other had filled it with hot coffee. 'Like you guessed, there was trouble. Some killer who shot down my brother after a card game. He wasn't even armed when it happened. This man lit out of town in a hurry, but left a trail I was able to follow. Turned out that he was the nephew of a big rancher down south. I caught up with him as he and a bunch of his men were rustling part of a herd from one of their neighbours. It was a fair fight, I called him out and killed him.'

Banner nodded his head slowly. The look on his face said that this was an old story, one which he had heard several times before, maybe in slightly different versions, but always with the same theme of greed and violence running through it.

'And then his uncle started out on your trail,' he said tightly.

'That's right. I figured I'd lost 'em, but they pinned me down in some mesquite underbrush, shot me up and left me for dead.'

Banner sat forward on the edge of his chair. His mouth tightened into a thin, hard line. 'Where was all this?'

'A place called Bender's Edge. Ever heard of it?'

Banner's smile thinned. 'That's about two hundred miles south of here. One of the frontier towns.'

'Two hundred miles,' said Wade slowly, thoughtfully. 'That's about what I figured.'

'You'd better rest now,' said Banner quietly. He rose to his feet, took the empty plate and cup away. 'You've been very ill. It's goin' to take some time to get your strength back.'

'I don't know how I'm goin' to repay you for this.' Wade sank back on the pillow.

'Think nothin' of it,' said the other quickly. 'I'm only too glad to have somebody around to talk to. Ain't many folk come here except to get broken bones fixed or have their cuts bound up.'

Wade nodded wearily. He was aware of the other going out of the room, of the door closing softly. Then he drifted back to sleep and did not wake again until the following morning.

In the long days that followed, Wade Halleran slowly regained his strength. The wound in his head healed and the muscles under his left shoulder knit gradually. Then there came a day when he was well enough to ride. Almost three months had passed since that day, when he had ridden into town on that railroad train. The spring had gone, turned into high summer. A dusty drought lay over Selina.

When Wade broached the subject of riding out, of heading south, Doc Banner gave him a taut, suspicious stare. Then he shrugged. 'I reckon you know your own mind, Wade,' he said quietly. 'But I hope you know what you're ridin' into. This *hombre* Everett sounds a powerful and unscrupulous man to me. I ain't sayin' he didn't think he had a reason for gettin' his men together and killin' you and I figure the law wouldn't hold him to be a murderer if they catch up with him and bring him to trial. But there's no doubt that if they know you're still alive, and that you're ridin' back there to hunt them down, then you're ridin' into big trouble.'

'I ain't overlookin' that,' Wade said tightly. He buckled on the heavy gunbelt. It felt strange after his being without it for so long. 'But this is somethin' I've got to do. They made me lose an arm. I aim to show them that I'm still able to take care of my own chores.'

'Suit yourself. You're as fit as you'll ever be, I guess. Though if you're as quick on the draw as you were then, is another matter.'

'That's somethin' a man never forgets. It just needs practice.' Wade's right arm still felt a trifle stiff but he forced it to work. He still had money, for Banner had refused to take anything from him for treating him and feeding him during the past three months and with the money he bought himself a horse, bridle, Winchester and ammunition.

Banner gave the coal-black stallion an appraising look, then lifted his head and gave Wade a direct stare. He laid a hand on the horse's neck. 'This is a good piece of horseflesh,' he observed. 'Best I've seen for a long while. He'll take you far. But if, somehow, word should get to Bender's Edge before you do, and word like this has a way of travelling far and fast, then you'll find they'll be ready for you by the time you get there. What chance will you have then?'

'I'll take care of that when it happens,' Wade said, with more roughness than he had intended. He saw the look on the other's face and went on slowly and quietly. 'I'm sorry, Doc. I guess I am just a bit edgy. I know you're only tellin' me this for the best, but there are things a man has to do or he doesn't stay a man. You see that, don't you?'

'Sure I do, Wade. I reckon if I was in your shoes, I'd be doin' just this, in spite of what any danged old fool tried to tell me to the contrary. But be careful. From what you've told me, these men won't hesitate to shoot you in the back.'

'I know what kind of critters they are, Doc.' He tilted back the brim of his hat, touched the butt of the Colt at his waist, then raked spurs along the stallion's flanks and rode along the dusty street of Selina, heading south and west. He rode the sun out of the east that morning, mile on mile, across the cracked, sun-baked beds of dried-up rivers and creeks, through brown scrub, burned and scorched by the sun, striving to suck the last drop of moisture from the arid soil.

As he rode he balanced himself in the saddle, knees gripping the horse's belly, his right hand flicking down for the gun at his waist, drawing it from the holster, sweeping it up, finger on the trigger, thumb on the hammer. He did the action methodically, forcing his fingers, hand and wrist muscles to work, ignoring the stiffness and pain in his hand and arm. Some day Hugh Everett would stand in front of that gun.

CHAPTER FOUR

Killer in the Brush

That night he made a small fire in a coulee where it could not be seen. He was now far enough off the main trails for the risk of anyone stumbling on him during the night to be small. He had hobbled his mount among the trees a short distance away and now it was chewing contentedly on the lush grass that grew around the tall trunks. Against the utter hush of the night the stars hung in their thousands, giving a pale, shimmering light and in the topmost branches of the trees, a little stray breeze ran, carrying with it the odd sounds of the night. He ate a little food, then put down his blankets and stretched himself out in them, some distance from the fire so that he was lying inside the ring of dark shadow beyond the fireglow.

He slept most of the night, waking when it was grey dawn. The fire was only ashes now and he did not waste time or energy building it up. Shivering a little, he got to his feet, strapped on the gunbelt with a little difficulty, then threw the saddle on to the horse and climbed into it. There was a deep-rooted anger and urgency driving him on now, something he could neither forget nor ignore. He rode most of the morning, rode through the heat of noon and did not rest up until early afternoon. The country hereabouts was wild and stony, full of deep crevasses that were filled with black shadow and he kept away from them. Once, from a high ridge, he saw the main stage trail off to the north but he had no desire to move towards it. The fewer people knew that he was alive and heading back to Bender's Edge, the better. As Doc Banner had intimated, even the desert here had eyes and few men rode across it without being seen somewhere along the trail, even when they saw no one in return.

Through scattered pine stands that gave sign of what was to come near the mountains that loomed purple on the skyline, he made slow progress, but coming out of the pines he pushed ahead hurryingly, knowing he still had a long trail to cover.

Later in the evening, mountain shoulders pushed down close to the trail he had chosen, cramping it, almost blotting it out altogether in places. He knew nothing of this stretch of country, but he felt no concern. Most of his life had been spent in the hills and on the trails that wound endlessly over the wide prairies. He was used to the deep stillnesses that lay on the mountains, when it was so quiet that one fancied he could hear God speaking out over the whole of creation. But half-way along the upgrade leading into the hills, around a bend in the trail that carried him into a small clearing, he came across a fire that was still warm and the discovery heightened the tension that had been building up in him all day. He was still, he reckoned, some distance from the Everett spread, but if word had got ahead of him, then Hugh Everett might have men out watching all the trails for him. It was conceivable that someone in Selina had recognized him, someone on the Everett payroll and he had ridden hell for leather to warn the rancher. Two hundred miles was a short distance in this frontier country, particularly with a railroad linking towns. Hugh Everett would ship beef to the eastern markets and most of it would go through Selina. What more natural than that he should meet buyers there, or send in somebody he could trust?

He quartered the camp, found the prints of two riders leading off to the south, into the undulating ridges that laced the uppermost stretches of the hills. Some of Everett's men? The thought entered his mind and in spite of any attempt on his part to dismiss it, stayed there.

His second night out and he camped in the lee of a low ridge. Here he made cold camp, not wanting to make a fire. There were too many trails twisting through these hills to warrant the risk. Stretching himself out, he smoked a cigarette and crushed the butt into the moist soil. There were pines growing along the edge of the ridge, riding the last faint red strives of sunset.

Lying there he tried to figure things out in his mind, hoping that he could get them to make some kind of sense. There were times when a man who lived with violence got a strange flash of insight, so that he was able to tell how things were going to turn out. It had happened to Wade Halleran once or twice in the past, but not now, not at this moment. No matter how he tried to guess what might bother him uncommonly, a sensation that things were not going to go right for him, that there was something he had not allowed for in his calculations and if he was not careful it might prove to be the undoing of him. Certainly he could not hope to buck all of the rannies who worked for Hugh Everett. But in this country men owed loyalty to the boss of the spread on which they worked. They would carry out his orders without question, be they inside or outside the law. But this state of affairs lasted only so long as the boss was alive. Once he was dead they would feel no compunction about riding on and leaving his death unavenged. If he could get to Hugh Everett, finish what he had to do, then he would be satisfied. He felt little towards the men who had actually shot him. They had been merely carrying out Everett's orders.

Smoking another cigarette he watched the faint paleness in the west diminish in brightness and then disappear altogether. The hills took on a dark, shadowed, anonymous look about him. The night softened all of the harsh contours of the ground and when the moon finally rose, on the far side of midnight, gliding slowly skyward, shedding its own light over the scene, he at last turned on his blankets and closed his eyes, hoping to get some sleep.

The high-pitched shriek of some animal, deep among the pines, woke him with a start and he jerked himself up on to his haunches, staring off in the blackness, his hand reaching out for the gunbelt, drawing the Colt smoothly from its holster. He listened to the sound which had undeniably alarmed the creature. Around him the forest was silent, utterly still, with only the faint, atrophying echoes of that shrill animal call of warning in the distance. He drew up off his blankets, stepped silently towards the top of the ridge, keeping his head bowed, so as not to show silhouette against the skyline and crouched down among the rocks and stones that littered this side of the ridge. A minute passed and then he heard two horses coming along the trail over the far side of the ridge.

Wade waited tensely, pondering whether to go back to his mount and bring the rifle, then deciding against it. Danger could come quickly if either of these two men suspected his presence there and were looking for him specially. Why the feeling that they were on the look out for him, and him alone, should enter his mind at that moment, he did not know. But caution was uppermost in his mind now as he tried to push his sight through the dark shadows, waiting for the first sign of movement.

From the endless quiet of the green forest, he managed to trace out the movements of the men. They had stopped their horses now, dismounted, and were heading in his direction on foot. This in itself was ominous. Unless they were trappers and that did not seem likely, it could only mean they were moving in on him, hoping to take him unawares, possibly that they had picked up his trail back along the ridge. This was, he now thought, remembering that feeling of uneasiness which had plagued him earlier that evening, what had been wrong. He had not expected word to have travelled so fast, or Everett to have been so quick in forming a plan to get rid of him before he was able to get to Bender's Edge. Had it not been for that nocturnal animal, somewhere in the brush, he might still be lying asleep back there at his camp, and this time these killers would not have made the same mistake again, leaving him for dead until they had made absolutely certain.

Moving silently along the top of the ridge, keeping well down, he reached a dead tree which had been blown out of the ground some time in the past and which now afforded him excellent cover from which to watch the patch of open ground in front of him. If those two men continued along their present path they would have to cross that stretch of moonlit, open ground. Shifting position had not been an easy matter. The stalking gunmen would be watching equally for any movement on his part.

Straining all of his senses, he realized with a faint sense of shock that there was only one man moving in on him from the front now. He could hear nothing of the other and sank back into the shadows, baffled. He should have expected this, of course. If they knew where he was, and who he was, they would not take any chances; they would split up and one would advance from the ridge, while the other would swing noiselessly around to flank him. His dilemma was that he could not keep his eyes open for both of them and while he was watching for the man in front of him the other could easily swing around and come upon his camp from the side, would then know that he was awake and out in the brush someplace and, forwarned, he would lie in wait until Wade was forced to open fire on his companion, thereby giving his position away. It was a tricky situation. He cast about him with narrowed eyes, hoping to pick out a glimpse of the other man as he broke cover either up or down the ridge from where Wade lay. In the moonlight, he reckoned it would be possible to spot the other a hundred yards on either side of his present position.

As he crouched there he listened to the wind moaning among the pines. It would sigh softly and then burgeon up into a hissing sound, sending grains of sand scouring along the rocks. It kept going through his mind: What would you do if you were either of these two men, trailing down a fast man with a gun?

The moon went behind a patch of dark cloud and a long, black shadow slid over the ground in front of him. Sucking in a gust of wind, he lifted the Colt, his finger bar-straight on the trigger, and waited. He saw the movement almost as soon as the moonlight faded. Clearly the other had been waiting for just that moment. The man was poised on the edge of the scrub, perhaps thirty yards distant, head thrust forward a little, twisting this way and that as he peered up and down the ridge. Wade strained to recognize the other, wondering if it was any of the men from the Everett crew that had been with Clem Everett, when he had caught them rustling those cattle. The man froze for an instant, threw a quick glance up at the sky as if trying to judge how long the shadow would lie over the ground. Wade had only a shadowed profile to study and at a distance of thirty yards, it was not yet enough. Very quietly, a carbine in his hands. the man glided forward. Wade could afford to wait no longer. Once the other got to his side of the ridge, there was too much cover for him to dive into.

Lifting the Colt, he sent a shot at the other, saw the man duck back swiftly into the bushes, twist as he hit the ground. The next second, two shots were aimed at him and he heard the slugs cut over the top of the deadfall, scattering chips of bark and wood on top of his head. He pulled himself low, waited.

A moment later the man called sharply: 'We've got you pinned down, Halleran. Best come out with your hands lifted.'

Wade remained silent. He could guess that the other was simply waiting for him to answer so that he could draw a bead on him.

A pause, then the voice came again: 'This is the law, Halleran. You made a mistake ridin' back to this part of the territory. There's a warrant been sworn out for your arrest on a charge of killin' Clem Everett. If you got any defence, reckon you can spill it all at your trial.'

There won't be any trial as far as I'm concerned, Wade thought tightly: *and as for being the law, that's a lie for a start. You're both Hugh Everett's men, and even though he claims to be the law in Bender's Edge, that don't make what you're claimin' to do legal.*

'You got ten seconds to come out with your hands elevated, Halleran. If not, then we'll come in to get you.'

Keep talkin', you're just tryin' to attract my attention while your friend gets into position behind me.

The other began to count monotonously, then broke off sharply as Wade sent another shot in his direction, judging where the other was from the sound of his voice. Simultaneously a gunshot sounded from the trees a little behind him and off to one side. There came a second lancing orange flame as Wade threw himself down flat. He knew now where the second would-be-killer was. It seemed that he had forced their hand, shooting at the first man as quickly as he had. Now they had both been forced to give themselves away before they were really ready. He sent a shot in the direction of the muzzle blast, thought he heard a man give up a loud yell, but could not be certain. Another shot from a Winchester, and a dagger-like sliver of wood peeled off the deadfall and shot over his head. Swiftly, Wade drew in his exposed legs and once the fading echoes had died away, the silence came on again, thicker and more ominous and tense than before. There was no called-forward threat from the hidden gunmen, there had been no warning at all, and Wade Halleran knew from past experience of such men that this meant they were not there to scare him off, to force him to turn back from Bender's Edge, but fully intended to kill him, there and then.

The seconds dragged themselves by on leaden feet and behind the tree Wade lay cramped and waiting. It was possible that he had wounded the man trying to flank him, but it might be fatal to assume so. No sooner had the thought crossed his mind than another shot sounded and wood and rock stung his face as the bullet struck less than three inches from his head. He winced instinctively, pressed himself lower against the ground. He was at a bad disadvantage here. Although under cover as far as the first man was concerned, the other man on his flank could take him if he moved himself by so much as a couple of inches.

Before another shot could come from either man he was wriggling along the side of the deadfall. There was a narrow gully at the very end of it and a moment later he slithered down into it. The movement had not drawn a shot from either man and he guessed that the manoeuvre had not been seen. Pausing for a moment, sucking air in between tightly-clenched teeth, he raised himself up suddenly, aimed across the open ground and fired three shots, patterning them so that they effectively bracketed the position where he guessed the man to be. The crashing echoes of the third shot were still chasing themselves among the rocks when he heard the hidden gunman cry out and this time there was no mistaking the sound. One of his shots had found its mark. There was a crash as of a heavy body falling into the long brush around the trees. Bending, Wade reloaded the six-gun, holding the weapon between his knees as he thrust the slugs into the empty chambers.

Swinging to face the second man he heard the other crashing frenziedly through the brush, moving away into the trees. A few moments later he saw the man, head ducked low, dart across a patch of open ground and throw himself into the trees on the far side of the ridge. Very carefully, Wade exposed himself. When no shots came from across the open stretch of ground he guessed that the two gunmen had pulled out. He made an elaborate and time-consuming crawl forward, was half-way to the trees on the far side of the ridge when he heard the sound of horses moving away down the trail. Getting to his feet, he ran forward, Colt held ready in his hand. Inside the trees he found the spot where the man who had been crouched there, had flattened the brush. Bending, he examined the spot, then drew back his hand, saw that there was blood on it and knew that the gunman had been hurt. He could barely make out the boot tracks in the dimness, but finally he found several spent rifle cartridges and more blood on the grass leading back into the trees.

Slowly he made his way back to his camp. All thought of further sleep was gone from his mind. He did not think either of those two men would be back

71

that night, but he knew that when daylight came every trail through these hills could be crawling with Everett's men, once the rancher learned that he had not been killed, that he was still headed for Bender's Edge. He decided to travel through the few hours that were left of the night. It was possible that this was the last thing they would expect him to do and he might just be able to work his way through and around them.

He rode downgrade for three hours. The moon continued its long glide to the west, now past full and when dawn finally brightened he was riding over a small plateau, with the plains in the distance, just visible at intervals whenever the trail swung to the edge of the hillside.

Hugh Everett's smile was a tight-lipped, mirthless skinning of his teeth. The arrogance that was part of him lived around his mouth and in his eyes as he said tautly: 'I warned that I wanted this man Halleran killed. Yet you ride in here and say that he took you by surprise in the hills.' His temper flared, yet he somehow managed to keep it under a tight rein. 'There were two of you, against a one-armed man – and you still weren't able to destroy him.'

'He was ready for us,' said Carringer tightly. He nursed an arm that had been torn by a bullet. 'Somethin' must've warned him we were there. He fired on us before we were in position or we could've killed him before he knew it.'

'Where is he now?' Everett demanded.

'Still there in the hills,' said Elmore harshly. 'My guess is that he'll wait there until nightfall before he dares to make a move.'

'Then you guess wrong. I know this type of man. He'll do the one thing we never expect him to do. He'll probably move by daylight. Take what men you need and scour those hills. Make sure that he doesn't get to

72

town alive. I don't care what you do, or how you do it. But I want him dead before sundown.'

'What about this arm of mine?' growled Carringer. Everett regarded him coldly for a moment, then said through tightly-clenched teeth: 'Ride into town and get it fixed up. And while you're there keep your eyes and ears open for anythin' you might pick up about this *hombre*. Just in case he slips through Elmore's fingers again like he did last night.' He shot a venomous glance at the other as he spoke.

Elmore flushed redly and for a moment the veins in his neck stood out under the skin. Then he fought control over himself, shrugged. 'He won't get away this time. I'll have every trail down from those hills watched.'

'Then get goin',' snapped Everett. 'While you're standin' here talkin', he could be headin' into town.'

'He'd wait up until dawn,' Elmore said confidently. 'Those trails are bad after dark. That one where we found him leads past the break just below the Old Fintry mine. If he tried that before it got light this morning, he'd like as not go ever the edge and break his damnfool neck.'

'If that happened it would save us trouble,' remarked Everett. 'But somehow I hope it didn't. I want him here, alive, so that he can die slow.' There was something unutterably evil in the way he spoke that sent a little shiver through Elmore's body. Watching the other out of the corner of his eye as he strode for the door, he felt glad that he wasn't in this *hombre*'s shoes. Something must have worked through Hugh Everett's mind during the past few minutes that he had been talking. First he had wanted Halleran dead, now he was insisting that he be brought in alive. He smiled grimly as he stepped out into the courtyard, blinking in the strong sunlight. Everett wanted Halleran alive, but he hadn't said how much alive.

Stepping into the saddle he called to the men standing near the bunkhouse, gave them Everett's orders, waited until they were saddled up and then led them out towards the hill trail leading east.

They reached the foothills shortly before noon, spread out to cover the trail that led down from the high ridges and also the minor tracks which spread out from it. Half an hour after arriving there Elmore was reasonably certain that he had every route covered and that if Halleran was still up there somewhere, making his way down, it would be impossible for him to get through the cordon of men unnoticed.

From his vantage point, less than a mile inside the hills, Wade watched the men ride in, pushing their mounts at a punishing pace in the heat. He could guess who they were and why they were there. Those two men who had tried to jump him during the night had ridden hell for leather to Everett with the news that he was still alive. Everett had wasted no time in sending out a bunch of men to stop him and now they would spread out and try to block every trail down from the hills.

He had stayed with the trail where he had camped during the rest of the night. There had been one particularly bad time when he had encountered a fresh rock slide just at the point where the trail narrowed and swung around a big outcrop of rock. On one side of him the ground plummeted for more than three hundred feet on to the rocky slopes below. On the other side it rose sheer in a rock face with scarcely any breaks. And then, rounding the sharply-angled bend, he had come upon this slide, a fault in the earth which had virtually blocked the trail.

For long moments he had debated whether to wait until it was light and he could see his position, or to go on and risk his neck in the hope of getting past the break and out of the hills before first light. Either way represented a big risk himself. If he waited the hills could be swarming with Everett's men by the time he reached the foothills. If he pushed on the odds were stacked against him. In the end he decided to chance it. Dismounting, he had led the stallion forward along a pathway that, in places, could not have been more than twelve inches wide. He heard the horse's flanks scrape against the rough rocky wall, heard its shod hoofs strike loose shale on the very edge of the trail. Gingerly, he inched his way forward, keeping a slack hold on the reins so that the horse was able to put down its head and smell the ground underfoot. The moon was hidden behind a thick bank of clouds and the night seemed darker than he ever remembered it. Most of the way he had to go forward relying on his sense of touch completely, unable to see anything clearly unless he was only a few inches from it.

It took him longer to negotiate the break than he had anticipated. At the end of an hour he was past the worst of it and able to mount up once more, relying on the horse's sense of balance and instinct to keep them on the trail. Twenty minutes after moving past the break in the trail, he saw the dim silhouettes of buildings off to one side and a moment later the trail widened appreciably and he saw that it led past some ancient mine-workings. They seemed abandoned, but he took no chances, skirting around them cautiously in the darkness, finding the trail again on the far side, following it over sharp switchback courses that led him higher through the hills until he reached a point where the ground levelled off and from then on he was moving downgrade. The stallion was a sure-footed brute, made more wary by his experiences with the rock-slide back along the trail, and it proceeded cautiously, pausing often when they came to a stretch where the ground dipped more sharply than usual.

Wade realized before long that the ground, even here, was deceptive. The wind, blowing up off the desert, was soft but cold and touched his forehead with an icy finger where sweat had formed just beneath the brim of his hat. In places the pathway dropped almost precipitously down the side of the hills, and he was not altogether free from doubt until, when dawn did come, he found himself moving parallel with a narrow stream that rushed swiftly down from the heights, winding its way through stunted bushes and trees. Thick vegetation grew along its banks, where the ground was moist and in the greyness he could see no sign of the trail continuing on the other side. He sat for a moment in the saddle, arm resting on the pommel, then made a cigarette, lit it and drew the smoke gratefully into his lungs. It took some of the cold away from his chest and he felt better. There was, undoubtedly, a better way of moving down from the high ridges than this. Somewhere along the trail, in the darkness, he had taken the wrong turning. But he was still headed west and now that he was moving downward, he guessed that the narrow trail which he could just make out through the vegetation on his side of the stream, would eventually lead him down out of the hills.

He had gone perhaps a hundred feet when the track narrowed even further and he was crowded to the bank of the stream by the thick, clinging vegetation. The trail angled lower and lower, still following, as far as he could see, the course of the stream and from the look of it, he judged that it had not been recently used and was possibly nothing more than a track cut out by the mules used by the miners to bring in supplies. As he continued, he grew anxious for the passage along this stretch of trail to be done with, but he rode the horse slowly, letting it pick its own pace, holding the reins slackly in his hand.

Now, still within sight of the river, he sat on a lone

spur of rock and watched the oncoming riders, spurring their mounts across the plain below him. He estimated there were ten or a dozen of them, too many for him to buck, but if they spread out to watch the trails leading from the hills, then he had a chance of slipping through the ring of men that Everett clearly hoped to place around him.

He began anew the labour of finding a trail down the slope and through the timber and brush. He wished to keep as close as he could to the edge of the ridge so that he might keep an eye on the men below him. He guessed that they had reckoned on him waiting until light before trying to move down that narrow trail with the break half-way along it and they would not expect him to have got as far as this already. It was something he could possibly turn to his own advantage.

Acting on impulse, he turned his mount, rode it into the swift-running water. The river here had a sandy bed and the rush of the current struck against the black stallion's chest as it thrust its way forward. The mount was tired, he could feel it in the way it slowed at times, but he pulled it on, ducking his head whenever the lower branches of the trees met above the water in a thick canopy of green. Here, because of the proximity of the river, the air was cool and filled with the aromatic scent of pine.

He thought of the men he had seen a little earlier, wondered where they were now and whether any of them were watching the river. He doubted if they would consider him coming along the water, but the possibility was there and it could be fatal to forget it.

The sound of a voice came to him suddenly out of the thick timber off to his right and he reined up sharply. The tone had been thinned and short and it came to him then that the river had carried the sound for some distance. Gently he edged his mount forward, no sound carrying except for the ripple and rush of water over the gravelly bed. Twenty yards further on he heard a rattle in the brush as though someone had thrust his way forward into the undergrowth. All this was to his right, somewhere out of sight, but the sound of the voices continued now and again, it was possible for him to pick out a few words, but he could make no sense of the conversation.

The sun had dipped a little from the zenith, but the heat was gradually beginning to pile up all about him. He rubbed the sweat from his forehead, blinking it out of his eyes. Both sound and voices came to him again, growing more audible, coming nearer. He dropped back towards the other bank, swung from the saddle, when it became clear that the men were moving slightly ahead of him, would see him if he continued to ride along the river-bed. He paused for a moment to debate the proposition. If he delayed, the rest of the men might begin to swing around hemming him in. If he went on he might bump into these men, two of them he guessed there were, although possibly more. It was one of those quick decisions a man had to make at certain times in his life, and his debate was ended immediately.

Slipping through the knee-deep water, he moved into the tangled brush on the other bank, gun drawn. Everett sure meant to have him killed, he reflected as he crouched down among the trees, straining every sense to pick out the faintest sound, the slightest movement. The thought was still with him when, moved through the bushes, he came upon a couple of horses tethered to a low branch.

He pulled up sharply, every nerve taut, strung tight within him. He could see no sign of the riders, guessed they were somewhere around. He let his keen-eyed gaze wander around the small clearing, got his feet under him, ready to make dash for the other side, then paused instantly. The two men came out of the bushes less than ten yards from where he lay. He noticed the thick-set figures, the broad, hard features, the fact that they were both smoking and had their guns thrust into their holsters. Evidently they were expecting no trouble.

They approached their horses, swung round with their backs to Wade, now so close that he could have reached out and touched them with his hand. The taller man grunted hoarsely: 'You reckon he's anywhere around these parts?'

The other man shook his head. 'By now he's over the other side of the ridge, maybe sitting in one of the saloons in town where we ought to be, instead of running around in circles in these goddamned hills, just because Everett figures he's still here. We're wastin' our time.'

'But if he is still here?' persisted the other, speaking around the cigarette in his mouth.

'Then he's a danged fool. He must know what he's up against. Could be that he's headed back east.'

'Could be.' The other shrugged, reached out for the reins of his mount. Wade made up his mind on the instant. This was the only chance he would get and it was clear that these two men were alone, guarding this trail. Reversing the gun in his fist, he stepped forward silently behind the others. One of the men seemed to sense his presence there, for he began to turn, swinging his head as Wade's arm swept downward, the butt of the Colt connecting with the back of his skull. Before the second man could turn, his hand snaking for the gun at his waist, Wade had spun the Colt, jamming the barrel hard into the small of the other's back. Harshly he hissed in the man's ear: 'Hold it right there, mister, or this gun goes off.'

The other ran the tip of his tongue around his dry lips, said throatily: 'What is this mister? Who are you?'

'I'm the man you're lookin' for, as if you hadn't guessed that already,' said Wade, his tone going softly quiet amid the tall trees so that it carried no further than the edge of the clearing: 'And if you've got any ideas of yellin' for help, forget 'em. You'll be dead before you could get the words out of your mouth.'

He saw the fractional slump of the gunman's shoulders although from the tight line of his jaw he knew that the thought of yelling had lived for an instant in his mind. 'Now let your gunbelt go, slow and easy. I don't have to tell you that I'd just as soon kill you as not.'

The other lowered his hands to the buckle, loosened it, then let the belt fall with a soft noise into the thick grass. 'You won't get out of here, Halleran,' he said thinly. 'There are too many men watchin' the trails for you. And even if you made it into Bender's Edge, you'd never get out of there alive. Everett is the law in town too, or have you forgotten that?'

'I've forgotten nothin',' Wade told him grimly. 'Now how many men are there in the hills watchin' for me?'

'Five or six,' said the other after a pause that lasted for a fraction of a second.

Grinning viciously, Wade thrust the barrel of the gun harder into the other's back, heard the faint bleat of pain that came from his lips. 'You're lyin', friend,' he said quietly. 'I saw you ride up around noon. Almost a dozen of you.'

'All right, so there were twelve of us. That don't make it any easier for you to get out of these hills.'

'Maybe: maybe not. Is Everett with you?'

'No. He's waitin' back at the ranch.'

'And your orders were to take me in dead or alive?'

The other shook his head slowly. 'Not dead,' he said tonelessly. 'Everett wants you alive. I figure he's got somethin' real nice planned for you. Clem was his only kin. All of that ranch was to be left to him when Hugh

80

Everett died. Now he's got nobody to follow him.'

'I reckon that Clem ought to have thought of that before he gunned down an unarmed man – my brother.'

The other was silent at that and Wade guessed that the men who worked for Hugh Everett had already known what sort of a man his nephew was. Without giving the other time in which to think, he lifted his gun and brought it down with a sickening crunch just behind the other's ear. The man collapsed without a sound into the grass beside his companion.

Wade was now banking on there being no other men watching this trail. Climbing back into the saddle he rode along the river's edge, eyes alert, but less than an hour later he had reached the wider trail that led out on to the plain. A swift, all-embracing glance over his shoulder showed him nothing of the other men scouring the hills for him and digging spurs into the black stallion, he rode over the dry, arid plain in the direction of Bender's Edge.

Inwardly he felt dehydrated and tired. He had had little sleep during the past two days and beyond the weariness lay a more unpleasant feeling that he could not define. He knew he could expect no help from anyone in Bender's Edge. Those who would have helped him were all too afraid of Everett to try and there would be plenty of men in Everett's pay watching every move a stranger made.

Twilight came, lingered on; and yielded reluctantly to night before he sighted the town. He debated whether to ride in openly, or to circle around it and come in along one of the narrow, twisting, rubbish-filled alleys. In the end he gigged his mount and walked it along the main street, tasting the dust in his mouth. Most of Everett's men would still be up there in the hills, continuing their futile search for him, unless they had already discovered the two unconscious men. There would not be many in town looking for him.

Besides, sooner or later, word of his arrival would reach Everett's ears and the other would make a further move against him.

He passed several darkened buildings, pushed his sight along the street. There were several horses tethered outside the saloons and restaurants, standing hipshot in the darkness, and one or two idlers on the boardwalks, who watched him curiously out of flat eyes as he rode by, but made no move against him. He was riding by the dark mouth of one of the alleys when a grizzled, white-bearded man moved over in his direction, paused by his horse and said in a low voice:

'Yonder in the alley, mister. She's waitin' down there for you.'

CHAPTER FIVE

Warning

Wade hesitated at the other's words. The old fellow looked harmless enough, but that was nothing to go by. He knew no one in this town. Even the few folks he had met on his last visit here weren't likely to remember him. Bending low in the saddle, he whispered harshly: 'Who wants to talk to me?'

'Miss Jennifer. She's Ben Kerby's daughter. She's waitin' for you down the alley a piece. Guess it's mighty important if she wants to see you.'

Wade narrowed his eyes, lips tight in a line of indecision. It sounded too much like a trap and yet there was a note of insistent truth in the other's voice, clearly noticed. He reached a decision. Jerking the Colt from its holster, he levelled it on the other's chest.

'Right, old-timer,' he said tautly. 'You lead the way – and remember, this gun is on your back. The first wrong move from anybody and you won't know what happens next.'

For a moment the other eyed him with a bright-sharp stare. Then he turned and trotted back into the darkness. Wade walked his mount after the other, keeping his eyes skinned, probing the dark shadows in the alley. Here it was as black as midnight and he could see scarcely anything beyond the few piles of rubbish that littered the place.

They had gone perhaps fifteen yards along the alley, when he said harshly: 'All right, that's far enough. What sort of trap is this?'

'It's no trap, Mr Halleran,' said a calm voice from the darkness. The girl stepped out into the open where he could just make out her slender figure. Then she moved up to his mount, laid a hand on the horse's neck. He could see her face as a pale grey blur and even in the dimness, recognition was immediate. It was the girl he had met on the street the last time he had been in Bender's Edge; the girl who had identified Clem Everett for him. Now her face was lined and serious, her brow furrowed over the clear, level gaze.

He lowered the Colt slowly, then thrust it quickly into the holster. 'I'm afraid I don't understand, Ma'am,' he said, puzzled. 'How do you know my name, and why do you want to see me?'

'I should have thought that the answer to your last question was obvious.' Her voice was still low and serious. 'There are too many men in town just waiting to get you in their sights. Everett has men everywhere.'

'They were up in the hills all day, searching for me,' he said grimly; 'but they didn't find me.'

83

'Perhaps not. But here in town, things are different. The hills are big and wide and there are a thousand places there where a fugitive might lie low, even with fifty men looking for him. Here, there are very few places where a man can hide, where Hugh Everett doesn't get to hear of it.'

'I still don't understand. I—'

She cut him off sharply. 'You came riding into town as if you hadn't a care in the world. You were seen when you were still five miles away. If it had been one of Everett's men who had seen you, then you might never have got here alive. Fortunately it was one of the men who works for me. He warned me of what might happen, of what did happen when you ran into Clem Everett. I can see why Hugh Everett wants to kill you.'

'Clem Everett was a cold-blooded killer who shot down my brother without warning, knowing that he was unarmed. I swore that I'd even the score and I followed him across five hundred miles of mountains and deserts to do it. When I finally caught up with him he was rustling cattle for that crooked uncle of his. That's how they've managed to build up a herd like theirs. By rustling it from the other ranchers in the territory.'

'That's what we've, suspected for a long time,' said the girl evenly, 'but so far we've never been able to prove it. We've lost several men too, shot in the back from ambush.'

Wade remembered the dead man he had found after escaping from Everett and his crew, the man whose horse he had taken in his ride for freedom, and nodded in understanding.

'Then your father is one of the other ranchers?' he said. It was more of a statement of fact than a question.

She nodded. 'We have the Lazy D ranch, a few miles north-west of town. We had five thousand head of cattle a few years ago, but slowly it has dwindled until now we have scarcely half that number. Most of the other cattlemen are the same. Only Everett's herd has increased in number.'

'That speaks for itself,' Wade said grimly. 'But why are you tryin' to help me? If Hugh Everett finds out, he'll not stop until he's destroyed you, and your father.'

'He's tried that before, but so far he hasn't succeeded. I don't doubt that he'll try again. The Everett crew are all hardened killers, chosen for their skill with a gun. If we're to have any chance against them we need as many men on our side as possible.'

'And that's why you want to help me.'

She hesitated, then nodded. 'You're not safe so long as you stay in town. On the Lazy D spread you would be comparatively safe. At least there wouldn't be the constant danger of a bullet coming from any dark alley.'

'And you think that you're big enough to stop them from riding on to your spread and takin' me?'

She listened to the grimness in his voice, weighing it carefully her eyes not once leaving his face. Then she spoke from the shadows. 'I'll be quite honest with you. We need you just as much as you need us. We can help each other in doing so, stop Hugh Everett from taking over the entire territory. Because that's what he means to do by any method he can.'

'I can understand that. But they tell me you've got no law here in Bender's Edge. How do you mean to fight Everett and his gunslinger crew?'

'We have men. If it comes to a showdown they'll fight.'

Wade smiled thinly, teeth showing in the dark shadow of his face. 'You think so? You reckon that when the time comes they'll step up against those gunmen?'

He saw the girl lower her gaze, knew that she was troubled, was perhaps a little scared, and trying desperately not to show it. Lifting her head, she studied him briefly and when next she spoke her voice was strangely bitter, but whether towards him or not, he could not be sure. 'You wanted to avenge a murder; and you did that. Because of what you did Hugh Everett has sworn to kill you. Yet in spite of that you ride openly into town. Maybe you're green, but somehow I don't think so. Only a fool or a very brave man, confident of himself, would do what you did a little while ago. My father would speak to the Town Council here and maybe get them to offer you the job of Sheriff. If he did that, and they agreed, would you be willin' to help that way?'

He shook his head slowly. 'Listen, Miss Kerby,' he said, his voice rougher than he had really intended. 'I've met men like Everett and his gunslingers before and I know how they act and think. I've seen every kind of killer there is, and believe me, the worst kind is one who's out to kill for revenge.' His smile was tight-stretched and bitter with memory. 'I guess I can say that from personal experience.'

He saw her eyes narrow a little, but before she could utter the words which were obviously balanced in her mind, there came an interruption. The old man who had moved to the end of the alley, keeping a sharp look out along the street, came shambling back.

'One of Everett's men in the street, Miss Jennifer,' he said in a low tone. 'I've noticed him before today. Rode in shortly after dawn, went along to get his arm fixed.'

'Who is it?' Jennifer Kerby asked sharply.

'Carringer.' The oldster lifted his head tautly, gave Wade a sharp glance. 'I did hear that he got a slug in it up there in the hills last night. Wouldn't have been you he bumped into, would it?'

Wade drew his brows together in a straight line. 'Could have been,' he observed. 'Two men tried to jump me on the trail. I know I hit one of 'em, there was blood among the trees when I moved up.'

'You'd better come with me,' said the girl quietly, but in a tone which brooked of no argument. 'This town is getting too dangerous for you. Carringer would not only be here to get his arm fixed. He could've had that done in an hour or so. He's staying in town to watch for you, just in case those other two men in the hills miss you.'

'That makes sense,' said the old man, head cocked a little on one side.

'All right, Seth,' the girl said. 'Get my horse and bring it here. Hurry!' She stepped back a little way and Wade saw her confidence and self-assurance return. Her face, in the dimness, was shadowed and soft. 'It is possible that someone else saw you ride into town and passed word to him.'

Wade nodded. There was a sudden movement at the end of the alley where it opened out into the main street. Whirling in the saddle, he peered into the gloom, saw the man who edged across the open end of the alley. At first he thought it was Seth, returning with the girl's horse, then he saw that the man was on foot, had a drawn gun in his hand, and there was a bandage of some kind around the other arm. In the same instant that the warning flash of recognition entered his mind, the man whirled, lifted his gun and threw a shot along the alley at Wade. The muzzle flash burned a crimson-blue in the blackness and the crashing echo of the gunshot blew the night apart into a thousand screaming fragments.

Wade heard the low hum of the bullet as it sliced through the air close to his head. The would-be killer did not pause to see whether his shot had gone home. Ducking his head, he ran out of sight across the mouth of the alley.

'Stay where you are,' Wade said tautly and slid from the saddle, ran forward, his elbow scraping along the rough wall along one side of the alley. Dimly he heard the girl cry out behind him, but whether it was a warning cry or one telling him not to go, he did not know.

At the end of the alley, Wade pressed himself in tightly against the wall. He could hear nothing, no breathing that would indicate the man was just around the corner waiting for him to show himself. Very cautiously he risked a look into the street. There were shadows all the way along it, but he could see nothing of the assassin. The silence lay deeper than ever over the town. As he allowed his gaze to probe every likely place where the other might be hiding, he wondered briefly why nobody had bothered to come out into the street to see the cause of the gunshot. Perhaps, he thought wryly, they considered it safer and more prudent to remain indoors.

Wade moved out of the alley, very softly, his feet making no sound in the spongy dirt. He was half-way along the front of the nearby building when the bullet's explosion battered the clinging silence once more and flying chips of wood struck him on the shoulder as the slug hammered into the nearby upright. The breath of the slug touched him and he dived full length on the slatted boards, jerking his head around as he fell. Out of the corner of his vision, he had seen the thin lance of flame; knew exactly where Carringer was now, crouched down behind a rain-water barrel on the opposite side of the street.

Glancing cautiously through the woodwork of the railings, he noticed that there was no place the other could run to if he were flushed out from his present hiding place, without exposing himself to half a dozen quick shots. He guessed that Carringer, in attempting to manoeuvre him against this side of the street had overlooked his own precarious position, believing he could drop him with a shot from the shadows. He wriggled forward a little, making no sound, dragging his body along with his arm and tremendous heaves of his legs. Inwardly he hoped that the girl would stay where she was as he had told her and that Seth would not happen along and try to butt into this gunfight. If he did, he might only get himself killed: and at best, he might make it more difficult for him to flush Carringer out of his position.

Wade waited, listening with a part of his mind for any other movement in the street. If he had guessed Carringer's character aright, the other would have but little patience when it came to outwaiting another fast man with a gun. It was going to be this waiting that would eventually break the other down.

At length he heard a faint sigh come out of the other. It was this sudden, desperate need for air which betrayed him and the man seemed to know it, for he suddenly leapt to his feet, threw three shots in rapid succession across the street as he started to run along the far boardwalk, boots scraping on the wood in his haste. It had not been a long wait. Carringer had far less pure nerve than many men Wade had met up with.

Balancing the Colt gently in his hand, he sighted it on the running man, squeezed the trigger, felt the heavy weapon jerk in his fist. He fired only two shots, saw Carringer stagger, lurch and then go down. Scrambling to his feet he moved across the street, came at the other, the revolver lowing on the target that lay as a dull, vague lump on the boardwalk. The man did not move and bending, Wade felt the limpness in him, knew that one or both of his shots had found their mark.

There was a part of a crowd on the street as he straightened up, walked back to the alley where the girl was waiting for him. He heard men's voices shouting and then saw a handful of them go forward and gather around Carringer's body. Jennifer Kerby came out of the darkness. Seth was with her, holding on to the reins of her horse.

'Is he dead?' she asked in a tight little voice.

He nodded. 'He was behind the barrel yonder, waiting to drop me as soon as I stepped out.'

He moved over to the stallion, swung himself up into the saddle. Across the street there was still a crowd milling around the dead man. While he waited for the girl to mount, two of the men across the street broke away from the main group and walked in his direction. Both were frock-coated, wore side-whiskers. They paused on the boardwalk beside him and one of them said to the girl: 'What happened out here, Miss Jennifer? Did you see it?'

The girl nodded, holding the reins loosely in her hand. 'That man is Carringer, one of Hugh Everett's gunmen. He fired on us in the alley. When Wade Halleran here moved out he tried to shoot him down from the other side of the street. It was a fair fight.'

'That isn't how Hugh Everett is goin' to see it,' murmured the other sadly. 'He'll be here as soon as word of this shootin' gets to him'

'I don't doubt it,' said Jennifer Kerby crisply. She half-turned towards Wade. 'If he comes looking for Mr Halleran here, tell him that he's at the Lazy D.'

'Do you think that's wise, Miss Jennifer?' asked the other man seriously. His face bore a sober expression. 'Everett can be a bad man when he's crossed. You don't have the men out there to back up your play if you decide to buck him.'

'We'll see what happens if it comes to that.'

Wade, listening to the girl, wondered if she felt as really confident of the outcome of a showdown with Hugh Everett as she sounded.

'Let's ride,' she said after a pause, glancing at him obliquely. 'Meeting up with Everett's killers on the Lazy D is one thing, meeting them here in town is another.' She touched spurs to her mount, rode out along the street without a single sideways glance in the direction of the men bending over the dead gunhawk.

As they reached the edge of town, Wade glanced at the girl out of the edge of his vision. Her face seemed set and hard, as though she were wrestling with her thoughts and he fancied that depression had seized her and chilled her spirit now that they were out of town and away from the others. Her eyes were fixed on the trail ahead, but seeing little of it, and her lips were lying close, compressed. They rode along a rocky, open stretch of trail and then ran on into thick timber. Here, the encroaching trees and the thick carpet of pine needles muffled the sound of their horses and the whole world seemed to lie on either side of them, quiet and still.

As he rode Wade wondered what her father would have to say when he knew the identity of the man his daughter was bringing home to the ranch. There was little doubt that the other had heard of him, would have heard how he had clashed with Hugh Everett. It might be that Kerby was not prepared to take the risk of having his ranch house burned down about his ears, his men shot up on the range and his cattle driven off. On the other hand, the girl herself had seemed utterly confident of herself. Had she made up her mind about this herself, or was it part of her father's thinking? Certainly, if the small ranchers wished to live in peace in this territory, without fear of having their cattle rustled and their crews shot up, then they would all have to band together and stand up to Everett.

They came to a summit of the trail where the trees thinned and in front of them the track forked, one trail dipping swiftly downward and twisting into the dark distance where the plain stretched away to their right. The other, the left-hand trail, wound upgrade, into rougher, rugged country. At the fork the girl stopped her mount, pointed along the downgrade track. 'That trail leads across the plain to the hills where Everett's men tried to trap you,' she told him. 'It also leads by a roundabout route to the Everett spread. I wanted you to know where it was. If Hugh Everett does decide to send his gun crew against the Lazy D, this is the trail he's most likely to use.'

'And this trail?' Wade nodded towards the other. 'It leads to the Lazy D?'

'Yes.' She gave a quick nod, turned her head a little to look back along the trail in the direction from which they had come.

'You think they may be on our trail already?' he asked, divining her thoughts.

'It's possible,' she admitted. 'Carringer wasn't the only Everett man in town today.' She said nothing more, but went on, crossing a short bare bench and then into more timber, climbing steadily. She rode more quickly now, as though anxious to reach her destination and Wade kept up with her, occasionally turning his head to listen for any sound of pursuit. More and more the girl seemed to have drawn back into her own private thoughts and for half an hour this was the way of it. Then the road entered a wide clearing and in the dimness Wade made out the shape of a log cabin and a small barn beside it. Somewhere in the distance a waterfall made a dully muted racket and the air here was thick with a cool dampness.

A trio of dogs emerged from the barn, came forward suspiciously, paused to regard the two riders. Then the door of the cabin opened and a man stepped out, a Winchester laid across his arms. Wade eyed the other curiously. One of the hill folk, he decided inwardly, men who came out here to be away from the rest of humanity. Invariably they wanted no further contact with the human race, preferring to remain on their own, shunning other men. He was a little under six feet tall, but thin to the point of gauntness, so that he looked taller than he actually was. His thin shoulders were stooped and he had the look of a man who watched every trail and was suspicious of everything.

'You're out ridin' late, Miss Jennifer,' he said in a low tone. His brows crept nearer and he muttered something to the dogs as they edged forward, turning them rapidly. They went back into the barn, disappearing from sight.

'There was trouble in town, Jeb.' She glanced sideways at Wade. 'This man is coming to the ranch with me, Jeb. His name in Wade Halleran. If he ever needs help, remember he's with us.'

'Halleran,' said the other musingly. 'Seems to me I've heard that name mentioned before. Must've been some time back though.'

'About the time that Hugh Everett's nephew was killed,' said Wade softly.

He saw the instant recollection in the other man's eyes. The woodsman nodded. 'That's right. So you're the *hombre* who shot Clem Everett. Can't say I blame you. Reckon the town ought to be glad of what you did for them. Trouble is that Everett can ride in and take over that town any time he likes. They all know it. That's why they won't back you in anythin' you want to do against Everett.'

His glance was a sharp-edged look. He was a man, Wade decided, who lived alone with his conscience and did everything according to it; and his conscience would be such that it would stand in the way of nothing if it proved to be necessary.

'Any men ridden this way in the past hour or so, Jeb?' the girl asked.

The other shook his head. 'You're the first along the trail since sundown. You want me to keep my eyes open after you've gone?'

'Yes, do that,' said the girl. She turned away and

rode out of the clearing, not once looking over her shoulder to see if Wade was following. He rode a little way behind her as the trail narrowed and in places they were forced to clamber over rocks that thrust themselves up from the bare, arid ground. Clearly this was not the type of pasture land that Hugh Everett would want. He must have grabbed off all of the best land for himself, leaving the rest to be shared out among the other ranchers. Now, however, probably following the death of his nephew, he had decided to grab it all. Unless the smaller ranchers banded together to fight, he would undoubtedly succeed.

Not for another two miles or so did the country change. The terrain became progressively flatter. The soil was more fertile, here and there was grassland where cattle could be grazed. It was difficult to see everything in the darkness and it was not until they rode through a gate in a boundary fence that the girl seemed to relax from her thoughts.

'Can that man back there be really trusted?' Wade asked softly.

Jennifer Kerby turned her head and looked fully at him. 'Jeb Weston is one of our oldest friends. He can be trusted to the end.'

Wade nodded. 'And back there, near the trail, he can act as watchdog for you.'

She smiled a little. 'You're definitely not green,' she murmured. 'I knew I wasn't wrong about you. You've seen your share of violence, haven't you.'

'I've seen more than enough to last me for a lifetime,' he said with a trace of bitterness to his voice which he could not hide. 'When I came here lookin' for the man who shot down my brother, I intended only to have it out with him on even terms, which was more than he gave my brother. Then I intended to ride on and leave this place for good. But because of who he turned out to be, it wasn't the end of the trail for me, only the beginning of another vendetta.'

'I warned you of the consequences that first night we met in town,' she said, as they rode down the lee of a low hill. In the distance Wade could just make out the yellow glow of lamplight in a window. They rode into the courtyard ten minutes later and even before Wade had dismounted, the door of the ranch house opened, throwing a yellow swathe through the night, and a tall, broad-shouldered man was silhouetted against the lamplight. There were other men near the bunkhouse off to one side, men who watched suspiciously until they saw the girl get down from the saddle and walk forward.

'This is Wade Halleran, Dad,' she called as they walked towards the tall man standing on the porch. I met him in town. Like you thought, he came riding in just after dark. There was some trouble but I'll tell you about it while we eat.'

Wade felt a little twinge of surprise go through him at the girl's words. Then her father knew of him, had maybe sent her into town to find him and bring him back with her. Certainly Kerby showed no surprise as he held out his hand and shook Wade's warmly.

'I can guess why you came back to Bender's Edge, Mr Halleran. I suppose if I were in your shoes I'd do the same. But these are dangerous men you'll find yourself up against. There is evil in them and Hugh Everett is the worst of them all.'

'I'm beginnin' to find that out for myself,' Wade said. He followed the other into the parlour. 'Was it some of your cattle that Clem Everett was ridin' off when I caught' up with him?'

The other nodded. He lowered himself into a chair, stretched out his legs.

'We've all been losing cattle. It's been goin' on for years now. Only Everett seemed to escape it.'

'Didn't you suspect him at all?'

'We did. But suspectin' a man of rustlin' and provin' it are two very different things. Besides, we lost men whenever they struck. When a man is shot down out of ambush, it isn't easy to get anybody to take his place.'

Wade's smile was a thin thing. 'I can imagine. They'd take to the trail leadin' over the hill and keep on ridin'.'

The other nodded his head ponderously. Jennifer came in with coffee and food, placed them on the table. Sitting down, she said to her father: 'Everett had some men in the hills watching for Wade. He managed to slip through them this morning and rode into town after dark. It was while we were talking that Carringer, one of Everett's men found us and tried to gun Wade down. There was a gun duel and Carringer is dead.'

'I see,' said the other heavily. 'There may have been other men in town who now know what happened. If so, then they'll get word to Everett tonight. If not, somebody may decide to ride out tomorrow and tell him. Whichever it is, he'll know very soon and we can expect him to come lookin' for you.'

Wade chewed thoughtfully on the bacon on his plate, washed it down with the coffee. He said: 'I don't want to bring you any trouble. This is somethin' of my own makin'. I don't have call to involve you in my fight with Everett.'

Kerby ceased to smile. 'You don't fully understand the position here, Halleran. We're in this fight with Everett whether we like it or not. We have no other choice left open to us now but to fight. Maybe if we'd banded together at the beginning we would never have had this trouble. As it is, it's like a slow-runnin' fuse led into a box of dynamite. Sooner or later it all has to blow up.'

'And you're ready to meet it when it does come? What about the other ranchers in the territory? How do they stand? Maybe when it comes to the showdown they'll back out and leave you to face Everett alone.'

'That's possible,' agreed the other. 'If it does happen, then we'll fight alone.'

'Do you know how many hired gunslingers he has to back his play? Forty or more. Can you match them? And every man a fast one with a gun. They only know the law of the six-gun and my guess is that Everett is keepin' the law off their backs so long as they work and fight for him. He has a tight rein on them all and none of them will leave him.'

The other sat stone-still in his chair, eyes half closed. He seemed deep in thought but presently stirred himself. 'There are times when a man has to fight for what he believes to be right. Sooner or later this territory is goin' to grow up. We won't always be a frontier town. The railroad will come through and the whole country west of here will be colonized. Then we'll have real law and order and men like Everett will be finished. But until then it's up to us to fight.'

Wade sat back from the table, his plate clean, the coffee mug empty. He felt better with some of the life and warmth back in his body. 'Stay with your convictions,' he said softly. 'I like what it is you're tryin' to do, although I doubt your chances of success. But if you want to see Hugh Everett destroyed, then that is what I want also.'

'Then you will stay and help us?' asked the girl. Her glance held his for a moment and a second's warmth ran between them. Then she dropped her glance. He had the feeling that she was still prying him, still trying to assess him for his worth. Curiously, he felt no anger at this. 'I'll stay,' he nodded.

'I'll show you to the bunkhouse.' She got to her feet, moved around the table and led the way to the door. Outside, in the yard, dust still lay in an invisible blanket in the air, touching his nostrils and the back of his throat. The stars were out in their thousands in the clear sky that lay over the hills, forming a misty glow all the way down the smooth slopes of the firmament. He took his horse and let it into the small corral, then followed the girl over to the long, low-roofed shape of the bunkhouse. There were five men in the bunkhouse as they went inside and Jennifer Kerby stood in the entrance and said quietly: 'Boys, this is Wade Halleran. He's got a personal score to settle with Hugh Everett, so he's signing on for us. He'll be riding out with you to the line camp in the morning.'

Wade nodded to the others, pegged his gear and took the bunk which the tall man whose name was Forsyth indicated to him. He sat on the edge of the bunk and rolled himself a cigarette between his fingers, licking the paper and then thrusting it between his lips, feeling the gaze of the other men lying steadily on him. Most of them seemed to be ordinary cattlemen, although there were gunbelts hanging beside each bunk. He could see that they were still not sure of him. but there was nothing hostile in their gaze.

Forsyth said softly, his tone weighted and measured: 'This grudge you got against Everett. Anything to do with that nephew of his who got himself killed in a gunfight some time ago when they was rustlin' our beef?'

'That's right.' Wade nodded, drew smoke down into his lungs, then let it out in twin streams through his nostrils. 'I was the man whn killed him.' He let the words fall into a muffling silence, aware that the girl had gone some moments before.

There was little surprise on the other's face, and he nodded slowly. 'I had that figured the minute I set eyes on you. And it was Everett's men who did that to your arm.'

'I ain't exactly blamin' them for it. They were only actin' on Hugh Everett's orders. His big mistake was in believin' them when they said I was dead. Sooner or later he's goin' to realize that to his cost.'

'We've lost a lot of men to Everett's crew.'

'How many of you are there?'

'Seven out with the herd at one of the camps. We're the rest. There were four others. One got himself killed when Clem Everett made that last raid of his on our beef. The other three faded over the hill. They won't come back now. They're too damned scared of what Everett is likely to do to us once he figures that the Lazy D is a menace to him.'

Wade sat silent, thinking of that, then he stretched himself out in the bunk, stubbing out the butt of his cigarette on the floor by the bed. Maybe here, with the Lazy D, he might get a fresh chance at Everett on more even terms than if he had tried to hide out in the town; but it would have to be done in Kerby's time and not his own. Here he was under a form of restraint and that was something he did not like. Still, he had given his word that he would stay and he intended to stick by it. Kerby was risking a lot keeping him here and the other probably knew it. Once Everett discovered where he was, he would try his damnedest to force Kerby to turn him over to him. Everett might have been content to let things go on as they were between the two ranches. But not if he discovered that Kerby was giving sanctuary to the man he was hunting.

Two hours after Wade pulled out of the ranch for the line camp, Hugh Everett and a small bunch of his men reined up their mounts on the low hill that over-looked the ranch buildings. They were tired men who had ridden far and fast since dawn. Lifting his hand, Everett sat tall in the saddle, staring out, tight-lipped over the smoothly undulating ground in front of him. It had irked him to hear that somehow Halleran had slipped through the cordon of men he had thrown around the trails leading down from the hills. He had wrought his rage on the two men who had been the cause of Halleran's escape, the two men who had been held up by him near the river and then knocked unconscious, not giving the alarm until well into the afternoon, when it had been out of the question to try to catch Halleran before he hit town, even if they had pushed their mounts to the utter limit.

Then Carringer had spotted Halleran in town, had tried to shoot it out with him, only to meet his own death on the boardwalk. The man must have the luck of the very devil, he thought tartly; but that luck was fast running out. One of his men had seen Halleran talking with Jennifer Kerby and there was word that the two of them had ridden out of town together.

Giving a little snort, he clenched his teeth tightly together, gripped the reins with tightening fists, until the knuckles on his fingers stood out whitely with the pressure he was exerting.

One of the men rode up beside him a moment later, lifted an arm and pointed towards the ranch buildings. 'You reckon that Kerby has taken him in, hoping to use him against us?

Everett nodded. Far off in the distance it was just possible to make out a small herd of cattle, grazing on the hillside. Everett ran a dry tongue over equally dry lips. Soon, he thought grimly, all of this would be his. He would own an empire that stretched for more than two hundred miles in any direction, containing ten or twenty thousand head of cattle. For a long time that had been the only purpose in his mind, the only thing driving him on. When he died, all of it would be left to his nephew. Now Clem was dead, shot down in his prime by that gunfighter who had ridden out from the north, gunning him down without a chance.

But this man, Wade Halleran, was close now; very close. If Kerby was hoping to sign him on the payroll as an extra gun if it came to a showdown, then he would soon be forced to change his mind. He reckoned he knew how to handle Kerby and that spitfire daughter of his.

'Let's ride down and get this business over with,' he said suddenly. 'I don't expect it will take long.'

In a tight bunch they rode down the hill, reining up in the courtyard. The dust raised by their mounts hung in a thick cloud about them. Everett did not dismount, but rode his horse slowly towards the ranch house, sat still in the saddle, until the door opened and Kerby came out, standing with his thumbs in his belt. The two men eyed each other warily and grimly for several moments, and then Everett said tightly: 'I hear say in town that you're shelterin' a wanted killer, Kerby. That true?' His tone made it plain that he knew it was true, but that he wanted to see whether the other would admit it.

Kerby let his gaze travel beyond Hugh Everett, to the other riders, seated seemingly carelessly in their saddles, some with open sneers on their faces. Then he swung his gaze back to Everett, locked it unflinchingly with his. 'Who I hire to work for me is entirely my own affair, Everett. I don't ask you anything about the pedigree of those men at your back.'

'What I do,' murmured the other softly, with a trace of menace showing through his tone, 'isn't the question here. This man you've signed on killed my nephew, shot his down from ambush and—'

'That's a lie, Everett, and you know it,' said the other sharply. 'Your nephew was rustlin' my beef when Halleran caught up with him. Your nephew was a killer, wanted for shooting down an unarmed man – the worst sort of killer there is.' He saw the red flush rising into Everett's face, but went on slowly: 'It was a fair fight and your nephew was beaten to the draw. You had your chance to kill Halleran when you sent your men into the brush after him like a dog.'

Everett sat wholly still in the saddle, his lips drawn thin and tight. His eyes changed, darkened with a deep-seated wrath and when he spoke, it was obvious he was holding himself in check only with a tremendous effort of will. 'I'm not goin' to argue with you, Kerby. I want Halleran and I want him now. Turn him over to me and there'll be no more about it. Try to keep him from me and you'll regret it very soon.'

'You threatenin' me, Everett?' Kerby faced up to the other, stepping down from the porch into the courtyard.

'This is just a friendly warnin',' said the other, turning suddenly cautious. 'Remember that anybody can get a drop on anybody else at any time. This range is big enough for the two of us. But so long as Halleran is here there can be no peace between me and the Lazy D. What is this *hombre* to you anyway, Kerby? Just another killer who's riding through. He won't stay with you when the time comes. He's got the law on his back and he'll run for cover the minute anything shows up. I've seen his kind before and—'

'You don't fool me for one minute, Everett,' Kerby said, cutting in on the other sharply. He deliberately kept his hands by his sides. 'You want Halleran for shootin' down that no-good killer nephew of yours. When you've got him, then you'll turn on the rest of the ranchers in this valley, run us out of the territory one by one as you did the others a few years ago. If you couldn't do it by rustlin' the cattle, then you'll probably try to burn us out.'

Everett stared down at the other for a long moment. There was a little echo of uncertainty in his mind as he watched Kerby closely. The man seemed to be playing his hand a little too cool. Was he so confident that Halleran could help him against his own men?

'You're a fool, Kerby, talkin' like this,' he said finally, very slowly. 'I can shoot you down here and now and you won't be able to stop me. Now I'm tellin' you for the last time. Bring out this killer and let's get this over with. If not then I'll—'

'You'll do nothin',' said Kerby tightly. 'Right now there are seven men in the bunkhouse yonder and each one of them has a carbine sighted on you and your men. Better keep your hands well clear of your guns or they may get the wrong idea and start shootin'. Since you killed that man of mine a month ago, these others have been in a particularly savage mood. I might not be able to stop 'em if you did try something.'

For a moment neither Everett nor his men moved. Then, one at a time, they began to turn their heads, following out the line which Kerby had indicated by the slow inclination of his head. There was a hiss of gently expelled air, almost like a sigh that passed outward from every man on horseback as they saw the grim-visaged men who had silently ranged themselves along the bunkhouse, near the entrance into the court-yard, barring any withdrawal of Everett and his men. Into the ensuing fateful silence, Kerby said softly: 'If you want a showdown here and now, Everett, you can have it. Reckon that for the peace and safety of this territory and the decent citizens in the town, I ought to give my men the order to shoot you where you are, but I'm not a cold-blooded killer like you. Better ride on out of here before I change my mind.'

Hugh Everett sat like a stone in the saddle, his face twisted into a sharp grimace. He did not make a sound for a long moment. Then, through thinned lips and tightly-clenched teeth, he hissed: 'This is a big mistake lettin' me go now, Kerby. Because I swear I'll break you for this. I don't aim to give you another warnin'. The next time I come ridin' here, I'll bring all of my men with me and then we'll see who plays the hand.'

'Get ridin',' snapped Kerby harshly.

Very gradually Everett pulled round on the reins,

drawing the horse's head about. He gestured to the men behind him, being careful to keep his hand well clear of his holstered, lashed-down gun. Moving across the front of the bunkhouse, he spurred his mount forward, not looking at the men who had stepped to one side, acting on Kerby's order. They still held their carbines in their hands, fingers on the triggers.

When Everett and the others had gone Jennifer Kerby came out of the house and stood on the porch, staring after the bunch of riders, now only visible as a cloud of dust close to the top of the hill where the trail vanished over the ridge. There was a worried expression on her clear-cut features, her brow wrinkled as she drew her eyebows together.

'He meant what he said, Dad,' she said eventually, soberly. 'He'll come back and do his best to wipe us out.'

'I know,' the other nodded. 'But this time we'll be ready for them.' He reached a decision. 'I want you to ride into town, then over to the Hardy's ranch. See if they'll join with us. They may send some of their men over. We have to band together if we're to stop him.'

Jennifer gave a quick nod. 'I'll get the buckboard out right away.'

'Take Abe with you, just in case you run into trouble on the way. I don't think Everett will do anythin' until he's got most of his men together. He's clever. He won't leave his herd unguarded, just in case any of us take the chance to bring some of our own cattle back. But even without those men, he can still bring enough guns to bear to overwhelm us if we have to stand alone.'

He turned back to the house, reached the door, then paused: 'Where is Halleran now?' he asked.

'He rode out with some of the others to the camp when the rest of the boys came in early this morning.'

Kerby's eyes clouded a little. He said softly: 'It might have been better if he were here. Even with one arm he's probably one of the fastest men with a gun this side of the border. I'll have one of the men ride out and let him know what happened here.'

He stepped into the house, closing the door behind him. Inwardly, he was more worried than he cared to show. One thing did not square this deal. Everett must have been absolutely sure he could crush any opposition, warning him the way he had of his intentions.

CHAPTER SIX

Capture!

The sun was lifting above the horizon when the buckboard rolled out of the courtyard and started along the trail to the hills. The two on the creaking seat rode in silence, with Abe watching constantly ahead, each side, and occasionally back towards the ranch. Over the top of the hill the route dropped into the broken flats, the dull, sandy, inhospitable country that lay to the east of the Lazy D spread, then angled left to skirt the shielded stretch of a canyon along a meandering sandstone wall that lifted from the ground in a sheer unbroken stretch of rock for close on a quarter of a mile.

Abe held the reins loosely in his big hands, giving the two horses their heads. Inwardly he was a little uneasy. He had seen the look on Everett's face when he had threatened to ride back and finish the Lazy D and he knew that the rancher had meant every word of what he had said; and that he had the men and the guns to carry out his threat. Out of the corner of his eye he was able to see the tight, fixed expression on the girl's face and knew that she was feeling the same way as himself, worried and apprehensive. There were things happening in this territory now that he did not like. He was as willing to use a gun as any man, but he liked to know why he had to kill and destroy. This feud between Everett and the other ranchers had been building up for a long time now. Bender's Edge and the surrounding country was like a vast powder keg, with a slow-running fuse attached to it. Maybe it had been this *hombre* Halleran who had lit that fuse when he had ridden here and shot down Clem Everett; maybe something else had been the cause. But whatever it was, there was no doubt in his mind that the showdown was not far off now and men were going to die with a surprising suddenness soon.

Unexpectedly, Jennifer Kerby said suddenly: 'You're a man who knows the world, Abe. What sort of a man do you think Wade Halleran is?'

He glanced at her for a moment, unsure of what she wanted him to say. He had the feeling she had already made up her own mind on that point, and was now seeking assurance from someone else. He shrugged, flicked the whip over the backs of the two horses as they moved up a steep incline in the rocky trail. The huge shoulders of rock closed in on them from either side, catching the sound of the horses' hoofs on flint, and throwing it back at them, oddly magnified.

'He's a man who knows how to handle himself,' he began slowly. 'I reckon that he's used to violence, knows how to meet trouble head-on, if it has to be met at all.'

'Do you think he's like most of the others? A killer at heart, a saddle-tramp, with the law on his neck?'

Abe considered that for a long, reflective moment, then shook his head. His eyes narrowed. 'I ain't sure what it is about him that's drivin' him on the trail he's followin'. Maybe it's just that he feels real bitter about what Hugh Everett did to him, about losin' his arm like that, I mean. Ain't much for a one-armed man to do in this territory. He seems cut out for the gun though. Maybe that's what makes him smell different from the others. There's somethin' kickin' him in the back. Pretty soon, unless he finds what he's lookin' for and deals with it, he will be one of the wild ones. That drivin' force is goin' to grow until he can't hold it any longer.' He gave a quick grin. 'Maybe I'm wrong though. Maybe he'll settle once this is finished – if he comes through it alive. There's a *hombre* around these parts who can move pretty quickly and cunning when he has to and I reckon he's goin' to do it right now.'

'You mean Hugh Everett.'

'That's right, Miss Jennifer. He's a real bad one that. He wants to grab off the whole of this range and I got the feelin' that he hates the town for lettin' Halleran ride out instead of holdin' him there after Carringer was shot on the street.'

'But the townsfolk had nothing to do with that.'

Abe's grin widened. 'I know that and you know it. But either Everett don't, or he don't want to. Either way, he's aimin' to fix things now and he knows only one way of doin' that.'

He flicked the whip again, cracking it over the horses' backs, standing a little on the creaking seat as the buckboard swayed from side to side over the rough, stony ground. They were almost at the top of the upgrade now. Ahead of them a handful of stunted trees grew out of the thin, arid soil, their trunks and branches twisted curiously to one side, thrown that way during the years by the endless breeze that blew off the desert lands to the right, shaping every growing thing.

There was a moment of shade as they topped the rise, rode down among the boulders. The rocky walls of the canyon fell away on either side and they were heading out into more open country.

Carefully, Abe lowered himself into the back seat, then jerked himself abruptly upright as the sound of a rifle shot shattered the clinging stillness, sent screaming echoes crashing among the trees. One of the horses reared as the bullet tore a ragged trail through the flesh on its foreleg. Instinctively, Abe thrust the reins into the girl's hands, reached down for the Winchester, lying beside him in the wagon. His fingers were just closing about it, lifting it from the floor, when a menacing voice from the rocks yelled: 'Pull up and keep your hands away from that gun!'

For a moment Jennifer Kerby contemplated ignoring the warning, made to slap the reins down on the horses, then paused as two armed men stepped out from the rocks twenty feet along the trail, rifles lined up on them. The buckboard came to a stop with a squeal.

'That's better,' said the taller of the two men. 'Now just drop that rifle over the side on to the trail.'

Reluctantly, Abe obeyed, eyes bright and sharp. 'What is this?' he demanded. 'A hold-up? We ain't carryin any money.'

The man grinned tautly. He motioned his companion down on to the trail. 'Hugh Everett has figured that maybe your old man will be a little more helpful if we take care of you personally,' he said to the girl.

The short man scrambled down the rocks, moving towards the buckboard. His lips were drawn back in a leer as he came up to the girl. 'Better do as you're told,' he said thinly. 'We don't want to have to hurt you.'

'You'll answer for this,' said the girl sharply. She shook his hand away as he tried to pull her from the buckboard. The other man stepped down and moved in. He said quickly: 'Get her, Ed, and let's move out of here. This is a main trail and there might be some of the

Lazy D men comin' along.'

Forcing the girl out of the buckboard, they motioned her to the edge of the trail. As they moved, Abe saw his chance, eased his right hand, hidden by his body from the men, towards the gun at his waist. He had it clear of its holster when the tall man, alerted by some sixth sense, whirled towards him. Before Abe could bring up the gun barrel and line it on him, the other had jerked up the rifle and squeezed the trigger. The shot caught Abe high in the shoulder, the blasting impact knocking him off the seat and hurling him bodily back on to the floor of the buckboard. Spooked by the sound of the shot, the horses jerked forward in the traces, stampeding along the trail, the buckboard swaying from one side of the track to the other. A wheel scraped an outcrop of rock at the corner where it bent sharply, almost at right angles, and with horrified eyes, the girl saw the wagon overturn, go over the edge of the trail, out of sight. There was the rending crash of wood splintering as it careered down the steep slope, then silence.

'You murderers.' She swung on the stocky man and beat at him with her clenched fists. The other dropped his rifle, then reached out and caught her wrists, holding them in a punishing grip, grinning down as he thrust his face close to her.

'Regular little hellcat, ain't she?' he said with a sharp, barking laugh. 'I wonder what Everett wants us to do with her when we get her to the cabin?'

'Never mind about that now,' snapped the other. 'We've got to get out of here. There may have been others followin' them. Bring her to the horses.'

Struggling futilely in the other's grip, Jennifer Kerby was dragged along the trail, up into the rocks, to a small clearing set a little way back from the trail where three horses were tethered. It came to her then that the men had obviously never intended to bring Abe along with them, that they would have shot him down without compunction. The runaway buckboard had solved that problem for them. Even if that rifle shot had not killed him outright, he could not have survived that crash when the buckboard had gone over the edge of the trail.

Under the watchful eyes of the two kidnappers, she was forced to mount one of the horses and a few moments later they rode out of the clearing and took a narrow, meandering trail that led up through the rocks, away from the main trail.

Wade left his mount ground-tied, moved towards the camp fire near the small wagon that brought in the supplies for the line men. Bunched in an irregular circle half a mile away, the Lazy D herd slept on a stretch of high ground. Three men were on guard, circling the rim, watching for strays moving out, keeping the herd bunched; and watching too for men who might come in riding and yelling, with guns blazing from any direction, seeking to drive off part of that herd, up into the hills, pushing it across the boundary fence on to the Everett range. There the brands would be altered and there would be no chance of proving that the cattle had been stolen.

Darkness had reached in out of the east and now covered the entire world. It thrust in from the far horizons, enhanced rather than diminished by the thousands of bright-shining starpoints that glittered in the deep sphere of night. Pausing before entering the circle of red firelight, Wade threw a quick glance all around him, watching the dark mass of the herd. There was still a vast and empty loneliness here for these men. And for many of them it was a fear-filled loneliness, never knowing when death would strike in a spurt of a muzzle flame out of the shadows.

A tall figure moved over from the rim of firelight. Wade turned his head, saw Forsyth moving towards him. The other paused beside him, stood silent, looking out into the night. 'It's too quiet out there,' he said after a few moments. 'Too damned quiet for my likin'.'

'You think there may be trouble tonight?'

Forsyth pursed his lips, hitched his gunbelt higher around his middle. He shrugged. 'Could be. It's the sort of thing that Everett would do. If he thought that Kerby had drawn most of his men back to the ranch to meet any challenge there, he'd come for the herd. I'm sure of that.'

'There are only six of us here,' Wade remarked.

A moment while the fire crackled in the near distance and a faint lowing among the herd broke the stillness. He could feel the tension in the air. In the far distance it was just possible to hear the guards crooning the low melodies that men have sung to cattle from the time the first herd was bunched and driven across a continent.

'Maybe they won't come,' said Forsyth quietly. He knew that his voice lacked conviction. 'If they want a fight we'll give it to them.'

Wade gave a quick nod. Soberly, he said: 'Fighting isn't good; and killin' is bad. I've had to do both in the past and I didn't like it.'

'Now that you've signed up for the Lazy D, you'll see more fightin' than you probably bargained for,' muttered the other. They walked back to the fire. Coffee and beans were ready and Wade sank down gratefully on to the grass near the tongue of the supply wagon, stretched out his tired legs in front of him and spooned beans and strips of bacon on to his plate, filled his cup with coffee from the boiler that was always kept going during the night. In an hour's time the guards would come in, cold, chilled to the marrow, would look for hot coffee to bring the warmth and life back into their bodies. Then it would be his and Forsyth's turn to keep watch over the cattle.

The fire was up, pulsing and blazing brightly. Morgan, seated on the far side of the leaping flames, licked a fresh bundle of kindling on to it, watched through veiled eyes as the sparks drifted high into the air, were caught by the stray breeze and whiled away down the darkness.

All too soon the hour was over and the three men were riding in from the direction of the herd. Forsyth pushed himself to his feet, moved to where his mount was tethered, motioned to Wade. 'Time for our chore,' he said evenly. He swung himself up into the saddle, waited for Wade.

Checking the cinch, Wade stepped up, held the reins loosely in his hand, nodded to Morgan, then gigged his mount to follow the other. The three men were riding into camp as they rode out: Forsyth and Wade rode in silence to the herd half a mile away, each man engrossed in his own private thoughts. While Forsyth circled around to the left, Wade rode on into the star-strewn night, sitting tall and straight in the saddle, eyes probing into the darkness that lay all about him, ears tuned to the deep and utter stillness, picking out every sound, ready to separate the normal sounds of the night from those which gave a warning of danger.

Behind him, he could just make out the flickering orange glow of the camp fire and the sight of it made him realize just how bitterly cold it was at night, with the wind blowing down from the hills on the far rim of the range. He remembered the trail along which Jennifer Kerby had brought him when they had ridden from town that night after Carringer had died. She had told him then that if ever Everett meant to ride on to the Lazy D spread, he would bring his men that way. Glancing about him, watching the stars, he tried to judge in which direction it lay, but at night, it was difficult to judge directions.

There was a faint stirring in the herd as he rode the

rim. The steers bellowed occasionally, then settled down once more in a completely inexplicable way. That was what made them so dangerous, he reflected. A man could loose off half a dozen shots in their ears and they might do nothing more than bellow in mild protest. A storm could break over their heads, with lightning walking the night and thunder booming overhead, and nothing would happen. Then, acting on impulse, at some sudden, faint sound, they would surge forward and there would be no holding them until they had run themselves out on the horizon.

The silence grew, was still and so deep that a man could reach out and touch it. He let his mount move slowly around the rim of the herd, eyes watchful, aware of the weariness and the coldness in his bones, but knowing that whatever happened, he had to stay awake. Midnight came, passed in starlight. Then a dark cloud covered the sky in the distance, blotting out the stars and the first faint shimmering of moonlight. Thunder boomed softly in the far distance, grew louder as the storm came closer. He eyed it with a tense apprehension. The herd moved uneasily. As though sensing the oncoming storm, a steer bellowed, lifting a roar of protest to the heavens, a roar that was answered almost at once by a shimmering streak of lightning and the thunder roll, crashing mightily among the gathering clouds. The first drops of rain, big and heavy, fell on to the crown of his hat. Within seconds the downpour came, drenching him to the skin. He hugged himself tighter in the saddle, bowed his head as the wind sent the rain slashing at his face, and forced the horse to move onward, into the teeth of the storm.

It was big and frightening, full of the primeval savagery that must have existed long before man came on to the Earth. Wade had ridden through worse storms than this, but never when guarding cattle, finicky beasts who might just start running at the wrong moment. It only needed a small thing to start them off and all hell wouldn't have a chance of holding them. He peered forward into the blackness from underneath the wide brim of his hat. His clothing clung to his body, chafing and irritating with every move in the saddle. He thought of the fire he had just left, of the warmth and dryness inside the supply wagon where, no doubt, the other men were now lying, out of the storm, merely listening to the thunderous, snapping fury of it. He cursed good-naturedly under his breath, paused as he saw the rider emerging from the blackness.

Forsyth rode up to him, bent forward in the saddle, raised his voice so as to make himself heard above the rolling thunder. 'At least this storm will make it unlikely that any of Everett's men will come tonight.'

With an effort, Wade grinned. 'We may have some-thin' just as dangerous on our hands if the cattle decide to go.'

Forsyth gave the steers a watchful, wary glance, hunched his shoulders forward, rubbing his arms where they were numbed and chilled from the wind and rain. 'If they do start, we'll just have to try to keep 'em milling around. That way we might just hold 'em.' The wind snatched at his words and a solid sheet of rain struck viciously at the two men. A steer snorted, rumbled angrily. Another took up the sound. For a moment, Wade felt sure they were going to go. Then, just as swiftly, they settled back again. He let the breath go from his lips in a long drawn-out sigh of relief.

Half an hour and still the storm rode overhead, and now all of the sky was blotted out by the clouds. Then, far off in the eastern sky a thin film of yellow showed; faint at first, but gradually growing wider and brighter. Wade lifted his head. Almost as he watched the sky cleared as if the curtain of cloud were being rolled back by some giant invisible hand. Stars showed again, big and bright, as if the rain had washed all of the dust and haze from the heavens. The moon emerged from the dark cloud, shone yellow as it drifted clear, sailing majestically across the dome of the sky. A distant lightning flash laced the sky to the west, but the answering roll of thunder was so faint as to be scarcely audible.

'It's over,' said Forsyth. 'For a minute there I thought they'd stampede.'

Wade nodded, felt in his pocket for the makings of a smoke, uttered a snort of disgust as he found that the tobacco was sodden. He thrust the pack into his pocket again.

There was one last rumble of thunder; and another sound that brought Wade's head jerking upright. For a moment he was not sure whether or not he had really heard it. Maybe his mind had been dwelling for so long on the possibility of Everett's men moving in against the herd that he was actually beginning to imagine things. Then he noticed Forsyth's head cocked a little on one side, saw him turn to stare out over the moonlit plain.

'Sounded like a shot,' he said tautly. 'It came from over there.' He pointed in the direction away from the camp.

'Get back and warn the others,' Wade said tightly. 'We may have been mistaken, but we can't afford to take that chance.'

For a long second Forsyth stared at him, then wheeled his mount as Wade made a savage, impatient gesture with his hand. He spurred off into the darkness and Wade gigged his mount forward, feeling the stallion, tired as it was, respond under him. He jerked his gun from its holster, gripping the reins with his curled fingers at the same time. He had long since learned to allow for his handicap.

115

Soon he reached a low outcrop of ground, moved into the moon-thrown shadow of it and waited. For several minutes he could hear nothing, but the faint sigh of the wind, through the long grass, rustling the branches of the stunted bushes that grew sparsely nearby. Had it been a shot he had heard or just a trick of the wind? Maybe he had been premature in sending Forsyth to warn the others of a possible attack. Still, it was best to be on the safe side when dealing with men like Everett and his hired gunslingers.

He turned his head, caught the sudden movement at the very edge of his vision, and gently pulled his head down again. The small band of riders had moved out of the dense shadow of a clump of juniper less than two hundred yards away. They had clearly not seen him, but were moving carefully forward, strung out now in single file. He could not make out who they were at that distance; but he did not need to know.

Without taking his eyes from the men, he edged his mount back a little way, waited until they were less than fifty yards from his vantage point, then drew a quick bead on the leading man. His Colt spoke twice and he saw the man jerk and reel in the saddle, but he did not fall. Gun flame leapt at him as the rest of the men pulled their mounts off the narrow, stony trail, scattering in all directions. Two of them thundered their mounts towards him, jerking guns from leather and firing as they came. He heard the bullets sing over his head as he bent low in the saddle. Swinging his gun again, he triggered it swiftly. One of the riders threw up his arms, clawed at the air as though reaching for something invisible above him. Then he pitched forward, hit the ground like a sack, rolling over and over before vanishing from sight in the grass. His companion, shot high in the chest, drew himself up in the saddle in a paroxysm of agony, even as death claimed him. He struck dirt with a sodden sound and the riderless horses plunged on, racing past the spot where Wade was hidden. The firing had swung round now as the Everett crew went down out of sight among the bushes. Wade's stallion bucked and reared as more slugs whined close to it, some ricocheting thinly off the nearby rocks. He fought to control the animal, kneeing it savagely as it almost threw him from the saddle. The Everett gunmen were yelling and cursing as they tried to pin him down, running in all directions and the red flashes of their muzzle blasts tore the night apart.

Dimly he could hear someone yelling hoarsely: 'There's only one of them there, goddamit! Ride him down!'

Wade realized the danger of trying to remain seated on a spooked horse and knew it would be only a matter of minutes at the most, before the gunmen plucked up sufficient courage to remount and ride out to encircle him. By now, he reckoned, Forsyth ought to have reached camp and warned the others. With a savage gouge of his spurs he fought the horse around and rode off along the lee of the rocks, bullets following him closely.

Now he concentrated on staying in the saddle. Behind him there was more yelling as the gunmen saddled up. Although they had been discovered, it was clear they intended to go through with their original intention of driving off some of the herd, maybe also trying to wipe cut the guards.

Half-way to the wagon he met Forsyth and the others. 'What's happenin' out there?' shouted the fore-man.

'Some of the Everett bunch. I dropped two of them, maybe a third. But by now they'll have saddled up again and they'll try to hit the herd. We have to stop them before they manage to stampede those brutes.'

'How many are there?' Wade had wheeled his mount and the others matched their horses with his.

'Half a dozen, maybe. Not many more.'

'Then we'll take 'em,' roared Forsyth. He waved an arm to the men with him. A gun flared in the darkness. It was followed by another. There wasn't any holding Forsyth and the others now. Wade raced his horse after them. In the flooding yellow moonlight it was easy to pick out the Everett riders. They were already cutting in from the rocks towards the herd, firing their guns in the air in an attempt to stampede the cattle.

Lead cut across the space between the two groups of men – whining lead that hummed over the plain. One of the Everett riders fell screaming from the saddle, hit the dirt and bounced twice before lying still, directly in the path of another horse. It was grim and bitter business, this trade of death – grim and cold and without mercy. The Everett gunslingers were hardened men used to the trade of killing.

Wade saw one of the men moving in towards the cattle, heard the great beasts roaring as the man fired at them, the light from the muzzle flashes in their eyes, half-blinding them. It needed so little to start them on the run. Wade fired three more shots before the hammer clicked on an empty chamber. Then, through the haze of gunsmoke, he saw that the gunmen were spurring away. This was something he had not bargained for. Only three men remained in the saddle, and one of them was reeling drunkenly with every step his mount took, swaying from side to side as he strove to hold on to the reins.

The fleeing men reached the timber with a couple of shots following them. There was one final spurt of fire from a rustler's gun, and then they were gone. Shaking his head to clear it, he laboriously reloaded his gun, then thrust it back into leather. Slipping from the saddle, he walked towards one of the men lying face-downwards in a small hollow. He turned him over with his toe. The bullet had hit him high in the chest, dead centre, and the wide eyes were staring sightlessly up at the moon as if seeing something beyond it. His chest was a bloody mess. Forsyth came over, stood for a moment looking down. 'Never seen this *hombre* before,' he said. 'Maybe one of the boys will know him.' As an afterthought, he went on: 'That bullet sure made a mighty big hole in him.'

Wade made no reply, rubbing his side where a slug had torn through his shirt and burned a fiery streak along his flesh. He lifted his head and let the cold night wind blow on his face. There was sweat streaked on his forehead, congealing as the air caught it.

Pouching his gun, Forsyth said: 'You reckon they'll be back, Wade?'

The other shook his head. 'Not with only three men. They'll keep on ridin' until they get to the Everett place. What Hugh Everett will do when he hears that they failed again, I don't know.'

They rode back to the camp fire. On the brow of the hill the steers still slept and Wade guessed there would be no trouble from them. Gulping down two cups of hot coffee, swallowing the scalding liquid hastily in spite of the way it burned his throat, he watched as Forsyth bandaged the arm of one of the men, wrapping the strip of cloth around it, where a bullet had ploughed into the flesh.

Slowly, the hours of the night paced themselves by. The moon lifted to its zenith, then slid down the long drop to the west. The stars brightened for a while as the moonlight faded, throwing long shadows over the plains, then they faded as dawn streaked the east with grey. Stretching his stiff limbs, Wade stirred himself, put fresh wood on to the fire, kicking it a little to get the glowing embers to burn again, then walked to his horse, climbed stiffly into the saddle, forcing himself to ignore the aches and bruises in his body. He swung out to the herd, checked that all was well, circled it as the dawn brightened and then rode back into camp. The others were awake, making up their bed rolls, cooking the breakfast over the fire.

He was, by habit, a quick-moving man, and he felt inwardly chafed at the slow movements of events. Certainly some of Everett's men had been killed during the night and that meant that when the showdown did eventually come there would be less of them to face. But this had not really affected Hugh Everett himself and it was the rancher that Wade wanted to find in front of him. He wondered now if he had been right in accepting Jennifer Kerby's invitation to sign on the Lazy D payroll. Maybe if he had stayed in town he might have had a chance at Everett before now. Here, away from the ranch, he had no knowledge of what was going on there. He did not doubt that sooner or later Hugh Everett would try to force Kerby to hand him over. When that happened, he was not sure how the rancher would react to this pressure.

'You figure we ought to ride into town and let somebody know what happened here last night?' asked one of the men after a pause.

Forsyth stared at him for a long moment, then said grimly: 'Reckon there ain't no one to tell. There's no law in Bender's Edge. If anybody rides out here from the ranch today, we'll give him word to pass on to the boss. If not, I reckon it can wait until the other crew comes out in a couple of days time.'

He settled his shoulders back against the wheel of the supply wagon and stared moodily into the fire.

CHAPTER SEVEN

Beginning of Revenge

Slowly, painfully slowly, Abe recovered consciousness. He lay for several moments trying to collect his thoughts. His only awareness was of the pain in his chest, as if a red-hot branding iron had been thrust between his ribs and was being twisted slowly in his body. He felt the sweat on his forehead, blinked his eyes against the terrible glare of sunlight that struck agonizingly at him. It was a long while before he realized what had happened. Then, with a rush, memory returned. He recalled the two men who had waylaid the buckboard along the trail a piece, of his attempt to draw on them while their attention was distracted by the girl, and of the spurt of flame from the muzzle of the rifle as one of the men had turned on him and shot him down from point blank range.

After that things were a bit hazy. He could remember very little. There were scattered fragments of memory buried somewhere in his mind, but he could not dig them out.

Mechanically he tried to move, felt a tremendous weight across his legs, pinning him down. Straining the muscles of his neck and shoulders, he forced his head up, an inch at a time, staring down at his body. The wreckage of the buckboard lay all about him, tilted at a crazy, unbelievable angle and the strong sunlight, reflected from the rocks, made it difficult for him to see properly. There was a red haze hovering in front of his eyes, fogging his vision. He rubbed his hand across his eyes, running the tip of his tongue over parched lips. His throat felt dry and there was the warm stickiness of blood on his chest. The slug had taken him high up under the left shoulder. It must have missed the vital parts by less than an inch, but he had clearly lost a lot of blood while he had been unconscious, and judging by the angle of the sun, it had been an hour or more at least.

Sucking air down into his tortured chest, he tried to form things coherently in his mind. Somehow he knew that he had to move, even if it cost him his life. Kerby had to be warned of what had happened, that Miss Jennifer had been taken by two of Hugh Everett's men, taken he knew not where. Inch by inch, he struggled to pull himself clear of the piece of wood that held him down. Sweat beaded his forehead, but he did not pause for a single instant, driven on by the knowledge that at that very moment Jennifer Kerby was in grave danger and he was the only one to know of it.

Gasping with the strain, he eased himself clear of the wreckage at the far end of the smashed buckboard. He guessed that the horses must have been spooked by the shooting and had raced off with the buckboard, only to send it crashing over the edge of the trail at a sharply. angled bend. By twisting his head round he was just able to make out the trail, some twenty feet or so above where he lay. As yet, he had not thought about how he was going to reach it, even if he did manage to free himself from the splintered wreck of the wagon. The exertion brought more sweat out on to his forehead and along the muscles in the small of his back. His wound too had opened up again and blood was soaking into his shirt.

Half an hour passed before he finally succeeded in wriggling free of the wagon. He was forced to lie for several minutes on the rough, hot rocks beside it, sucking air into his lungs, getting some of his strength back for the long climb that lay ahead. At last, he dared to trust himself far enough to ease his way on to his feet, clawing at the rocks with both hands, digging in his fingers into any crack that gave him purchase to lever himself off the ground. Even when he finally got himself on to his knees the battle was not over. He had to fight to stay there, to battle against the rising nausea in the pit of his stomach, against the blackness of unconsciousness that threatened to seep out of the sun-blazing rocks and engulf him once more. It would have been so easy to lie down on the rocks and surrender himself to the weakness and the unconsciousness. Then his mind would remember the girl and he would force himself to struggle on, exerting all of his waning strength as he strove to climb up the steep slope to the trail. The sun beat down on him mercilessly from the cloudless heavens, burning his back and shoulders. His hat had been lost somewhere and without its protection, his head ached and there were long moments when he scarcely knew what he was doing and why.

Somehow he made it to the top, paused for a moment with his arms hooked over the hard, rocky edge of the dusty trail. He hung there for what seemed an eternity, before he had summoned up sufficient strength to haul himself over on to the trail itself. He lay face-downward, gasping for air, the dust stinging his nostrils, clogging his mouth and throat. His chest was hurting again and it was a long while before he was able to claw his way across the trail to the far side, where the rocky wall lifted for a few feet above the track. Sitting slumped, with his shoulders against the sun-baked rock, he forced himself to breathe slowly and evenly. His heart was thumping madly in his chest, hammering painfully against his ribs as if it would burst asunder with the tremendous strain. Squinting up at the sun, he guessed that it was a little after noon. The shadows were short and the heat-head had lifted to its maximum intensity. Every breath he sucked down into his lungs burned like fire and he tried weakly to spit the gritty taste of the dust from his mouth. There had been a canteen of water in the buckboard, but by now it would be lost somewhere among the rocks down there. Weakly he rubbed his legs where the rough wood had chafed his flesh.

The sudden movement along the trail, less than fifteen yards away, caused him to jerk his head around, his right hand dipping towards the gun at his waist. He relaxed as he saw the horse move into sight. It was one of the two which had been harnessed to the buckboard. Somehow it had become separated from its companion and instinct had made it wander back in the direction of the ranch. With an effort he jerked himself away from the rock wall, ignoring the pain which lanced through his torn body. The red mist returned to waver in front of his eyes, but in spite of this he somehow staggered to his feet, calling upon all of his reserves of strength. Weakly, he whistled the horse up, waited until it had trotted up to him, then put out a hand and patted its neck, leaning on it as he did so. The horse snickered faintly, muzzled against him for a moment as if aware that he had been hurt. It made no move to shy away and he held his breath as he felt for the reins. There was no saddle on the horse and he would have to make it back to the ranch bareback. But he had no choice in the matter.

Murmuring softly to the animal, he somehow swung himself up on to its back, leaned forward over its neck. 'All right, fella,' he said softly. 'Let's get back. But take it easy, boy, all the way.'

As if it understood every word he said, the horse

started off along the rough, winding trail, jogging along at a slow, but steady pace. Gripping its mane, he forced a tight hold in the thick, silky hair, hanging on with all of his strength.

The journey seemed endless. He lacked the strength to guide the horse, but by some uncanny instinct, it seemed to know the route back to the Lazy D for some time later, it moved down into the dusty courtyard, paused in front of the corral. Abe lay over its back, his breath gushing harshly in and out of his lungs. Then he heard the babble of voices, as if from a great distance, and above them all, Kerby saying:

'Get him down off that horse, boys. And be careful how you handle him. He's been hit bad by the look of it.' Abe felt strong hands lift him from the horse. Unable to help himself, he relaxed utterly, surrendering to the weakness that overwhelmed him. He was only dimly aware that he was being carried into the house, set down on the couch there and there were dark figures hovering above him, their faces little more than grey blurs, details and features unrecognizable. They seemed to move towards him and then recede to a great distance in a manner which was both alarming and puzzling. With an effort he blinked his eyes, tried to focus them on the men around him.

'Just lie still and we'll get the Doc to take a look at that wound of yours, Abe,' said Kerby. His voice was tight and there was an unasked question in it. Then he went on: 'What happened out there? Where's Jennifer?'

Somehow, Abe forced his lips to shape the words. At first they were only a soft mumble that made no sense, then he got them out more clearly: 'Two of Everett's men jumped us on the trail some way from here, up near the pass. They took Miss Jennifer away and shot me when I tried to draw on them.'

'You got any idea when this happened, Abe?'

'Must've been a couple of hours ago; maybe more. Hard to tell out there.'

'Sure, sure. Now just you lie there and take it easy until the doctor gets here. In the meantime, I want you Slim, to ride out for the camp and warn Halleran of what has hampened.'

'Halleran just?' said Slim.

'That's right. This may sound wrong, but I figure him for the fastest gun here and if we're to get my daughter back without any harm coming to her, it'll be a job for just one man. Send in a bunch and they'd likely kill her out of hand, rather than let us get her back. But one man might be able to follow their trail and get up on them unawares.'

Slim nodded, left the parlour, went outside. A moment later there was the sound of a rider spurring his mount at speed out of the courtyard. Hiding his worry and impatience, Kerby stood looking down at the badly injured man on the couch. It was little more than a miracle that the other had managed to make it back to the ranch with the news. The other, he thought, must have been half dead when he had regained consciousness in the wreckage of the wagon; yet somehow he had succeeded in freeing himself and getting back.

The day had been long and hot but now that the afternoon was almost over the air was cooler. An earlier breeze that had sent gusts of dry sand scudding over the rangeland from the west had died and the air was very still. They had seen nothing more of Everett's gunmen on the spread and for three hours, acting on his own impulse, Wade had ridden the boundary fence with the Everett range, keeping his eyes open, but although he had seen a cloud of dust way off in the distance a little before high noon, the riders had not come any closer and he had watched them carefully out of sight. That Everett was laying some plan against the Lazy D was obvious; and he only wished that he had some inkling as to what it was. He found it more and more difficult to control the impatience in his mind. He had ridden here to finish things with Hugh Everett and so far nothing had happened. If Kerby did try to buck the Everett crew and failed, then he was right back where he had started; no, worse than that, for now Everett knew where he was and why he was there. The element of surprise was gone, possibly for good.

Turning his mount, he rode back in the direction of the camp. Hunger gnawed his belly and the long day had begun to tell on him. Mounting a rise, he could make out the camp in the distance, just visible, perhaps five miles away. There seemed no point in hurrying, there was only his hunger driving him on, and he let his mount pick its own pace.

Events soon proved otherwise. He was still half a mile from camp when he saw the lone rider head out in his direction. From the way the other was riding, he guessed that there was some kind of trouble. Digging his heels in, he urged his horse forward, a tightening sense of apprehension in his mind, knotting the muscles of his stomach. The man rode up to him, said harshly: 'You'd better get back to camp fast. Slim just rode in from the ranch. There's been trouble.'

Wade asked no questions, but dug rowels into the stallion's flanks. He felt sorry for his mount as he did so, but there had been something in the other's voice . . .

Dropping from the saddle on the run, he looped the reins over the stallion's head and strode towards the camp. Slim was standing by the wagon. He glanced up as Wade arrived.

'What's this about trouble, Slim?' Wade asked tautly.

'Kerby sent me to fetch you in a hurry, Wade,' said Slim quietly. 'It's Miss Jennifer. She's been kidnapped by two of Everett's men. Abe got in a little while ago with a bullet in his chest.'

Wade sucked in a sharp breath, then nodded, swung back to his mount, drew himself up into the saddle. All thought of food had gone from his mind now. 'Let's go,' he said sharply to Slim.

They rode out fast, spurring their mounts at a punishing speed. The news had come as a distinct shock to Wade, yet the more he thought of it, the more logical it seemed that Everett would do something like this. If he could not beat Kerby down by mere threats, he would force the issue.

Less than an hour later they rode into the courtyard of the ranch. Kerby was sitting on the porch as they rode up and got to his feet at once as Wade dismounted and ran forward across the yard.

Kerby's features were drawn and tight. He seemed to have aged ten years since Wade had last seen him only a couple of days before. He said harshly: 'Slim will have told you what happened, Wade. You've got to find my daughter for me.'

'I'll do my best. But why me?'

'I figure you for the best man for the job. You're fast with a gun when you have to be and I reckon you're used to the ways of violence. The men I have on the ranch are only cowhands.'

'May I talk to Abe?'

The other gave a quick nod. 'I doubt if he can tell you any more than you already know. The doctor has seen him and says he's damned lucky to be still alive, but that he'll pull through OK.'

Wade followed Kerby into the house. Abe was lying on one of the beds, his face white and bloodless, his body naked from the waist upward. There was a broad bandage around his chest with the faintest hint of blood showing through where the wound was still bleeding a little in spite of everything the doctor had been able to do. He gripped the iron bars at the end of the bed with both hands, knuckles standing out under the skin as he pulled hard whenever a spasm of pain went through him.

'Howdy, old-timer,' Wade greeted. 'You got any idea who these men were?'

'Two of Everett's gunslingers. That's all I know. Never saw either of 'em before in my life.'

'How'd you know they was ridin' for Hugh Everett?'

'Heard 'em say that Hugh had ordered them to take the girl someplace where she'd be safe until the boss had decided to do as Everett said.'

Wade nodded. He did not doubt the truth of the other's words. But it was always wisest to know what one was up against before riding into trouble. 'And when did it happen?'

'Around eleven o'clock, I guess. I got back here as soon as I could, but with that lead in my chest it weren't easy.'

Wade gave a quick nod, got to his feet. 'Reckon you'd better rest up now, Abe. I'll ride out and see if I can pick up their trail.' He moved to the door. Outside Kerby joined him a little while later.

'I've sent a couple of my men to the other ranchers in these parts,' he said tightly. 'That was what Jennifer was goin' to do when they kidnapped her. We shall need all the guns we can get if Everett attacks; and my guess is that he'll do it soon. He knows that he can't afford to wait, just in case the others do come in with me.'

'Then you still mean to fight him even though he does hold your daughter as hostage?' For a second, Wade felt a sudden sense of surprise. He had expected the other to back down in the face of this new development.

'I must. It's what Jennifer would want. Believe me, I don't like the idea of possibly sacrificing her, but the

129

whole of the frontier is goin' to depend on destroyin' men like Everett.'

'And if the other ranchers won't throw in their hand with you? What then? You'll be destroyed. That's for sure.'

'I'm bankin' on them joinin' me, on them realizin' that their continued livelihood depends on finishing Everett once and for all. Just as I'm dependin' on you to get to my daughter before they carry out their threat.'

'I'll do what I can,' Wade said grimly. Moving to the door, he opened it, paused, gave Kerby a bright-sharp stare. 'One thing though; Everett is mine.'

Kerby nodded wordlessly. From the bed, Abe said thickly: 'A word of warnin', Wade. Watch those two critters. They're as wary as a couple of coyotes. They may have smeared up their trail to stop anybody from followin' them.'

'I had that figured. Any ideas where they might have taken her? You know these parts better than most.'

'The hills there are full of places where a couple of men and a girl could hide up,' said Abe after a short pause, ruminating on the question. He looked at Wade with a moment's penetrating attention. 'That trail leads past Jeb Weston's shack. Maybe he saw somethin'. Check with him first. If anyone knows the likeliest place where they're hidin' out, Jeb's your man.'

'That's right,' Kerby nodded agreement. 'And he can be trusted. I'll stake my life on him. He'll never be bought off by Everett, or scared off either.'

Wade reached his horse, made a wide circle of the ranch, then headed up into the hills. He reckoned there were still three hours or more to sunset and with luck he should reach the point along the trail where the kidnapping had occurred. He pushed his mount as he rode, his mind spun into a tightening web of purpose.

He did not question Kerby's assessment of the situation. If a bunch of men rode out looking for the girl the chances of them being seen were too high and those two gunmen might kill her out of hand, rather than face a noose. When he got into timber, he traced his way along the winding, meandering trail, through the green gloom under the trees. Here he was above the plain and able to look down and see for a long distance. Nothing moved down there on the stretching smoothness and there was no dust hazing the air to indicate that other riders had preceded him.

The stillness was heightened by the utter absence of movement. This, he felt sure, was a signal of things to come, which the hills and the timber heeded by its suppressed quiet. He thought of Jennifer Kerby as he rode, wondered a little about her. Somehow, the thought of her brought a sense of warmth and satisfaction to his mind, superseded by anger at what Everett had done.

He ran three miles through the hills before he finally came out on to the narrow stretch of trail that wound up in front of him, dropping out of sight just beyond the narrow pass. He recognized the spot instantly from Abe's description and moved off the trail just over the summit. Two minutes and he discovered the place where horses had been tethered recently. The prints in the ground indicated three animals; evidently the two kidnappers had not intended taking anyone else with them except the girl.

Picking up the trail, he followed it at a lope, keeping his eyes on the ground ahead of him, noticing a broken twig here and a crushed clump of rough grass there, each tiny point as clear to his keen-eyed gaze as if it had been written there in the dirt. The trail became rougher as he ascended into the foothills of the narrow range. Here and there he encountered wide stretches of smooth, weathered rock on which no print showed and he was forced to scout the further edge to pick up the faint trail once more, losing precious time as he did so.

Splashing across a shallow stream, he followed the tracks along the bank and up through a clearing. From there the men and the girl had gone downgrade again and judging by the appearance of the prints in the muddy ground near the bank of the stream, they had been in a hurry. Whether they expected pursuit to be rapid, or were taking no chances, he did not know. But the thought that their hide-out might be some considerable distance away, worried him. It would be dark soon and impossible to follow the trail. He did not wish to have to camp all night, starting out at first light the next morning. Too much time had already been wasted since those men had taken the girl. It was just possible, of course, that they had taken her straight to Everett's place. If they had, then there might be very little he could do. But inwardly, he felt certain that Everett had wanted her out of the way, holding her as his ace in the hole until he saw how things were going to pan out. If Kerby decided to fight – and at the moment that seemed to be his decision – then the girl's chances of living were considerably diminished.

Moving steadily through a brush patch, he followed the tracks to the end of the bushes. From here he noticed that the tracks angled sharply to the left, back in the direction of the main trail. Puzzled, he followed them through the waning light of early evening. It was strange that they should have headed in this direction, especially if they knew of Jeb Weston's connections with the Kerbys. Jennifer had warned Weston to keep a sharp look out for anyone moving along the trail and Weston looked to be the kind of man who could take care of himself when it came to a showdown.

Rounding a bend in the trail he began to catch glimpses of the waterfall which he had heard close

beside the log cabin when he had headed this way with
the girl. The faint thunder of its fall reached him a few
moments later and he saw the mist among the trees
where the warmth of the day had drawn the dampness
from the ground. Then, ahead, he saw the roof of the
cabin nestled, among the trees, dipped down along the
trail and reined up in front of the shack. There was no
sound from inside the building as he dismounted and
moved quietly towards it. He knew how quick these
mountain men were and wanted to take no chances on
the other shooting him before he could yell out that he
was a friend.

Reaching the door, he rapped loudly on it with his
knuckles. Still no sound, then he heard the faint rustle
in the brush at his back, whirled, saw the rifle levelled
on him and kept his hand well away from his side.

Jeb Weston moved forward across the small clearing, then lowered the weapon as he recognized him. He
said gruffly: 'Thought you might be another one of
them critters.'

'You see anybody headin' in this direction any time
durin' the afternoon, Jeb?' Wade asked quickly.

'Sure did,' affirmed the other. He pointed a finger
towards the ridge that ran athwart the trail some two
hundred yards distance. 'Spotted 'em headin' along
that ridge about two hours ago. They seemed in a
mighty hurry and I recognized the horses. They were
Everett's men.'

'How many?'

'Three. Though come to think of it, one did seem
different. Could have been that—'

Grimly Wade broke in on the other, his tone cutting
through the stillness like the lash of a whip. 'That was
Miss Jennifer,' he said. 'Those two *hombres* took her off
the buckboard back there along the trail, shot Abe in
the chest. You got any idea which way they went?'

He saw the look on the old man's face change subtly.

When he spoke again there was a deep anger in his voice. 'Miss Jennifer, you say?' His grip on the stock of his rifle tightened perceptibly. 'You goin' after them?'

'That's right. Now, do you know where they might be headed?'

'That trail yonder leads back into the hills, towards the old silver mines. Don't go any further once it gets there.'

'You're sure of that?'

Jeb nodded his head quickly, emphatically. 'Course I'm sure,' he said harshly. 'Besides, you won't have too much difficulty followin' those two. I winged one of 'em.' He patted the Winchester meaningly.

'That might slow them up,' Wade acknowledged. He lifted a hand, swung back into the saddle, rode up through the trees, intersecting the higher trail ten minutes later.

Presently he recovered the tracks of the three horses. At first the marks were easily read, but as the ground grew rougher and more stony, the prints were less apparent. Often he was forced to go on without a sign to follow, choosing one particular path through the rocks rather than one of the others, because to any rider it would have seemed the more direct and as he guessed, these men were in a hurry. Particularly now that one of them was hurt, it seemed the logical thing for them to do.

Half an hour after leaving Weston, he rode down into a narrow, rocky defile and stopped his mount in the deep shadow of it. The sun was westering rapidly now, drooping almost perceptibly towards the dark horizon. He started out again, then drew back rapidly as he became aware that the trail broadened, here and there were buildings of a sort along the slope directly ahead of him. Narrowing his eyes against the red glare of the setting sun, he perused the scene in front of him, watching for any sign of life. Several seconds passed before he caught a glimpse of the horses tethered high along the slope. He felt a sudden sense of relief at the knowledge that he had managed to track them down while there was still a little daylight left.

There was a wealth of shadows lying over the ground in the wide canyon where the trail had been gouged out of the hill some years before. Most of the buildings left there did not seem safe to enter, their wooden walls tilted at crazy angles where age or ground subsidence had shifted them from their original foundations. A ghost town, he thought, maybe fifteen or twenty small cabins which had been occupied at one time by the men who had mined the silver from the veins in the hillside. But the miners had long since pulled out when the lode had run out, leaving the place for wanted men, for killers with the law on their trail.

He was mindful of the fact that two pair of eyes might be watching the trail, alert for any pursuit. Somehow he had to find a way of getting close enough to see what was going on, without being spotted himself. A quick glance was enough to tell him that this was not going to be easy. The ground was open in front of him. Then too, the nearest of the shacks was more than a hundred yards from him and all of the way he would be exposed to fire from the other shacks. He slid from the saddle, hobbled his mount out of sight behind the rocks and sat with his shoulders against the outcrop of stone, feeling the night chill draw in about him, pondering his next move. Loosening his holstered gun, he let his hand rest lightly on it, tracing out in the growing darkness the line of the trail as it wound up from where he sat, to the far end of the small mining village.

The rocky walls on either side were high and virtually unscaleable, even for a man with two arms. For him it would be out of the question to get up there and then lower himself down near the mouth of the mine workings. He drank some of the water from his canteen, occasionally moving his head to peer around the side of the rocks, keeping a close watch on the cluster of shacks.

He knew that he was reasonably safe from observation here in this tumble of huge boulders unless anybody happened along the main trail and that did not appear likely.

The shadows came, stealthily long and thin at first, then swiftly growing wider and deeper as the incoming night nibbled away at the last vestiges of light in the heavens. The sun vanished in a vast, silent explosion of flame far below the horizon and the air cooled swiftly. Wade remained for a long time, watching the shacks, seeking any sign of life, knowing that sooner or later one of the men would have to put in an appearance. He took care not to show himself. The two men may earlier have considered themselves to be safe, with Everett probably pulling the strings around the Kerby range, but since Jeb Weston had seen them and fired, injuring one of them, they would be more scared, and frightened men had sharp eyes when it came to watching for any sign of pursuit. Leading his horse into a small clearing off the trail, he hobbled it, then crawled to the edge of the vast outcrop of rock which had been his hiding place for almost two hours. Now the fates which had seemed to be against him wearied of their sport and came to his aid. There was a faint orange glow, just visible against the encroaching darkness, a glow that undoubtedly came from a fire in the last shack but one along the trail. It was, he reckoned, only natural that the men would have chosen one of the furthest shacks in which to hide out. From there they would have more warning of any impending attack.

There was still a great depth of quietness around him and in the middle of it he could distinctly hear the harsh sound of his own breathing. Edging forward, he pressed himself tautly against the smooth rock, blending his body with it so as not to be seen from the shack. The fact that they had chosen one furthest away from the trail would make it easier for him to move forward unseen. He cast a swift look about him, noticed the row of rusted wagons that stood on the brown rails less than thirty yards from him, off to his right. If he could make them without being seen it was just possible that he could move forward to the nearest shack. Once there he would have to formulate a plan for getting closer to the shack where the others were hidden. Setting his wary course for the wagons, he slid forward, making no sound in the deep dust that lay everywhere. Some time in the past rock had been pulverized here to extract the last grains of silver from the ore and now it lay over the ground to a depth of almost two inches. It formed an excellent muffling carpet.

Crossing into the shadows of the wagons he pressed himself down into the dust. So far there had been no indication from the shack that his presence had been detected. Easing his way along the line of wagons he studied the open ground which lay between him and the foundationless miner's hut that stood some sixty feet away. Taking out his Colt, he cocked it, made to move forward into the open, then paused sharply as a door in the distance creaked open. Lifting his head, he was just able to make out a shaft of flickering orange light and briefly silhouetted against it the tall figure of one of the men. The other muttered something to someone inside the shack, then stepped out and made his way along the trail to where the horses were hobbled. Wade waited until the other was out of sight, then darted across the open stretch of ground to the shack. There was a glassless window in one side and the door hung open on sprung hinges. One side had sunk into the earth so that he had to stoop to get inside.

The man came back less than five minutes later,

went back inside the shack at the end of the trail. Wade settled down to wait, knowing that it would be fatal to rush in, that it needed only one bullet from either man and Jennifer Kerby would be dead. Somehow, he had to get one of those men away from the girl. A probing glance told him that apart from the door there was only one window to the shack where the two men were holed up with the girl, and that it would be possible for him to move along the backs of the shacks without too much risk of being seen.

Narrowing his concentration, he eased his way towards the slanted door of the shack, bent to edge out into the night, then paused, a faint chill of apprehension going through him as he heard the unmistakable sound of an oncoming rider along the trail. A sharp hiss of breath passed through his lips. Whoever it was heading onward at a rapid rate, it could only be one of Everett's men. Anyone else would be more wary in their approach.

He listened intently as the rider came on, then heard the horse slow, rein up while still a short distance away from the entrance into the mine workings. He cursed himself inwardly. The rider must have spotted his mount out there, had possibly recognized it. There was a pause while the silence built up, grew more tense, then the horse came forward once more, more slowly this time and glancing down the trail he saw the rider move into the open. The distance and the darkness were too great for him to recognize the man; but a moment later the rider yelled: 'Ned! Bob!'

There was a sharp, answering shout from the distant shack, but Wade scarcely heard it; for the rider coming slowly along the trail now was none other than Hugh Everett! What could have brought the other out here? he wondered tautly. Worry, in case this chore had somehow been bungled? A desire to see for himself that he still held the upper hand in spite of the fact that his attempt to run off part of Kerby's herd and destroy his guards had failed miserably.

'Come on up, boss,' shouted the man. 'We're up this way.'

'Anything wrong?' Everett was wary. He had undoubtedly seen that horse and he was worried now, knew that he might be the target for some hidden marksman, crouched among the multitude of shadows.

Wade gritted his teeth until they hurt, the muscles of his jaw lumping under the skin. Why not shoot him down now and get it over with? he told himself fiercely. He might never get a better chance and he felt confident that he could handle those two polecats at the shack. Then he remembered the girl, knew that her life could easily be forfeit if he tried anything like that. He lowered the gun, held his breath until it hurt in his lungs as Everett came riding by, a dark shape in the night, the sound of his mount the only noise to break the utter stillness. Wade let him go, watched closely as the rancher moved along the slope and reined up outside the shack where one of the men stepped out to meet him.

'You're sure there's nothin' wrong?' he heard Everett say, his tone suddenly sharp, edged with concern.

'Should there be? We ran into that old coot Weston on the way here and he plugged Bob in the arm, but I've bandaged it up for him and—'

'There's a horse hobbled back yonder, down the trail a couple of hundred yards away. It's Halleran's mount. There's no mistakin' that black stallion.'

'Halleran!' Ned jerked out the single word as though unable to trust his ears. 'Then he must be somewhere in the shacks by now.'

A pause, then Everett's voice went on: 'I doubt it. If he was, he'd have taken a shot at me as I rode by. I figure he's scoutin' the place, lookin' for a way in without bein' seen. He'll be more wary now after seein' me

139

arrive. Leave Bob here to look after the girl. Even with a hole in his arm I figure he ought to be more than a match for her. You'll take that side of the trail and I'll take the other and if you see any sign of Halleran, shoot to kill. You understand?'

Ned's reply was lost to Wade, but he could guess what it had been. He looked anxiously at the shadowed shacks on either side of the trail, then along to the rearing walls of rocks and knew that he was boxed in. He had no time now to back out and head back, for already the two men were moving out into the shadows.

CHAPTER EIGHT

Revenge

Moving to the rear of the shack, Wade hunted around, found the rear door, little more than a square hole in the side of the hut, criss-crossed with pieces of wood. He eased them away, the nails which had once held them in place, rusted and broken, crawled through, making as little noise as possible. There was the faint sound of somebody moving along the shacks to his left and wasting no time, he bent, scooped up a handful of the sharp pebbles and tossed them as far as he could, heard them hit among the rocks twenty or thirty feet away.

There was the roar of a gun blast and the sound of a voice yelling harshly. 'He's over this way, boss. Up in the rocks.'

Even before the atrophying echoes of the gunshot had died away, Wade had run around the side of the shack, out to the front, waited while the rancher raced across the broad trail and vanished among the shacks where Ned was crouched. Less than fifteen seconds later, Wade was down among the shadows on the other side of the trail.

Everett's voice came down from the far side of the mining camp. 'Where the hell is he then? Did you hit him?'

'I'm not sure. I heard him move up there and fired at him.'

Everett said impatiently: 'Well he ain't there now, unless he's skipped into the rocks. Better pull your fool head down in case he decides to take a shot at it. I reckon you must've been shootin' at shadows.'

There was a long silence, then in a rough, pained voice, Ned said: 'He's got to be around here someplace if you saw his mount back there along the trail.'

There was a long pause and Wade strained his ears to pick out where the two men were. From his hiding place he could see the shack with the yellow light shining behind the window and could smell the smoke from the wood fire that they had started. He tried to guess at the other men's actions. Now that they had fallen silent he guessed that Everett had decided Ned had been tricked and he had warned the other to circle around, to move towards the end of the building line, to try for a fair shot at him if he ever exposed himself in the open.

Therefore Wade continued to inch forward until he reached a spot where he could look along the whole length of the trail and still keep his eye on the shack where the girl was being held prisoner. He knew that Everett would not have her harmed until he knew what was happening at the Kerby place, and also until he had found Wade Halleran. He would not feel safe with him wandering around in the night.

At the corner of the low-roofed shack, he stood debating. If the two men had split up again, with one edging along the far side of the line of shacks opposite him and the other cutting back towards the trail, they would sooner or later have to cross the trail. If they didn't cross they would be lying in wait in the shadows, or crawling into the tumble-down shacks for a surprise play. There was no way of knowing. He could wait here and hope to break their nerve – make one or both of them move and betray their position. Or he could do the moving himself and start hunting them down in the darkness.

Gently he eased the Colt up and down in its holster a few times. It was not in him to wait for long. This showdown had been hanging fire too long for him to be patient. The knowledge that Everett was out there somewhere, not too far away, drummed through his mind, forcing him to a decision.

Turning, he slid about the building, peered into the deeper darkness that lay among the shacks on the far side of the trail, thought he heard one of the horses in the distance snicker softly and his head jerked round sharply at the sound. Had Ned or Everett gone crawling off in that direction, possibly knowing he was watching the trail and so moving further out than he had anticipated, moving back over the trail somewhere out of sight? If that was the case he dismissed it from his mind at once. Both men would not carry out the same manoeuvre and now he had his chance to get them separately. He noticed Everett's horse, standing patiently in front of the shack, paused in the darkness to catch his breath and listen.

The next three shacks on the far side of the road were very close together and he doubted if a man would be able to squeeze between them now, with the walls having sagged over the years, pressing them tightly together. Then, close at hand, something stirred and he heard the faint sound of a body pushing forward through the clinging dust, the soft metallic clink of a gun catching on the wall of one of the buildings.

He began to smell the dust dragged up by his own feet and it came to him that the other men would probably smell it too and track him down, knowing where he was. He looked to left and right, discovered nothing. Then, at the very edge of his vision, he saw the man step across one of the narrow openings on the other side of the trail. It had been only a brief glimpse, but it was enough for him.

Sucking in a heavy gust of wind he withdrew the revolver from its holster, stepped soundlessly across the street. The emptiness around the buildings diffused any sound of movement so that it was hard to know just where the other was. Wade got to the front of the shack pressing himself against the warped wood of its timbers. He edged forward slowly, holding his breath. Then he heard the other man breathing, a harsh sound in the stillness. Carefully he reversed his gun. The man was doing a strange thing. He was backing away now, moving along the wall in Wade's direction, his gun out but pointing in the other direction. Then the other stopped, was on the point of turning his head when the butt of Wade's pistol struck him just behind the ear. The blow made a dull, soggy sound and Wade caught the other's body with his arm as the man sagged to his knees, head dipping forward, falling on to his face in the thick dust.

Shaking the other with his hand, he satisfied himself that the man would be unconscious for a long time. He bent lower to stare at the other's face. It was one he did not recognize, evidently the man called Ned. That meant that Everett was still out there somewhere, scouring the place for him. He smiled grimly as he got to his feet. Maybe Everett did fancy himself as a gunfighter and a man had to be hard to keep a bunch of killers like these in hand, but somehow Wade doubted if he had the courage to face up to him in an even fight. That meant he would do his best to shoot him in the back if he gave the other half a chance.

Wade moved cautiously forward towards the screening darkness along the side of the trail. He heard the snicker again from the horses tethered up near the entrance to the mine shaft, heard them stirring a little. To a man used to the ways of horses he knew with a sudden certainty that Everett was up there, still working his way around the shanty town. His smile broadened for a moment, became in ugly thing.

He crossed the stretch of ground to the shack where Bob was guarding the girl. He had already made up his mind what he was going to do next. At each in-between space he paused and looked along it to the front of the building – to the road along which Everett might try to come. He put his head against the wall of the shack and heard the low speaking of one voice and then another, the latter feminine and defiant. One dull lance of pale yellow light showed through a wide crack in the wall and moving closer, he was able to make out Bob's harsh tones.

'Now just you sit right there and you won't get hurt. As soon as your friend Halleran is finished, we may be ridin' back to the Everett spread. I figure your Pa will know what he has to do if he wants to get you back alive.'

'You won't get away with this,' declared the girl. 'Wade Halleran is out there now, somewhere in the night and for all you know, Everett and your friend are dead and he's drawing closer to you.'

'You ain't scarin' me none,' snarled the other viciously. 'Now keep your mouth shut if you know what's good for you. Everett said you was to be kept

144

alive, but he didn't exactly say how much alive.' There was a veiled threat in the other's words that sent a little shiver through Wade's mind. Gripping the gun more tightly in his fist, he worked his way along the wall of the hut, approached the front door. The place where the horses were tethered was more than two hundred yards away and in the dimness he could see nothing moving there. If Everett was striving to edge his way across he trail, to come up on him from the rear – believing that Ned was still around, hoping to trap him between two guns – then he was keeping himself well out of sight.

Pressing himself in against the edge of the door, finger bar-straight on the trigger, he placed the toe of his boot close against the bottom of the door. Bob was talking again, and Wade could hear him moving around. The door was not completely shut and for a moment he caught sight of the other's shadow as he moved in front of the door, between it and the lamp. Wade waited no longer. Kicking the door open with his foot, he crashed inside, the barrel of his gun levelling on the man's chest. The other swung sharply, said: 'That you, Everett—' then let his words dribble away into a stunned, unbelieving silence.

The girl, tied to a chair near the table, uttered a glad cry. There were dark bruises on her face and a smear of blood on one cheek. Her gaze held his for a moment, then she said sharply: 'Wade!'

Wade saw the man's sudden sideways swing, saw the black muzzle of the gun lifting sharply on him. There was a vicious grin on the man's face, a look almost of triumph as if he sincerely believed that he had beaten the other to the draw.

Almost dispassionately, Wade squeezed the trigger, loosing off only the one shot. The burned powder bloomed blue-crimson in the dim lamplight and the din crashed back from the walls, magnified by the confined

145

space. In the racket he heard Bob cry out, a loud and terrible cry, saw him stagger as the slug hit him in the middle of the chest, just below the breastbone. Bob's eyes widened in stunned surprise, then the expression faded from them and they began to glaze over. His mouth opened, muscles suddenly slack as he tried to get words out, but they refused to come. Instead, there was simply a harsh, inarticulate grunt, and then a rush of red that dribbled down his chin as he buckled at the knees and fell forward, the drawn Colt sliding from fingers that were suddenly useless, lacking even the strength to loose off one shot.

Stepping swiftly forward, Wade passed his hand over the top of the lamp, extinguishing it immediately. In the darkness, he moved to the door, glanced out into the night. He heard the girl say breathlessly: 'There are two more, Wade. I think one of them is Everett. It may have been his voice I heard shouting a little while ago.'

'It was,' Wade said grimly. 'He's out there somewhere, wondering what has happened. I caught up with Ned at the back of one of the shacks. He's likely to be unconscious for quite a while.'

A couple of seconds later he saw the dark shape dart from behind one of the boulders strewn on the higher slopes overlooking the mining village, out near the entrance to the mine itself. The echoes of that solitary shot were still clattering among the higher reaches of the hills, fading swiftly. Everett vanished from sight, but now Wade knew where he was and that gave him the advantage. Going back into the middle of the room, he thrust the Colt into his belt, pulled out the sharp, long-bladed Bowie knife, felt for the thongs that held the girl prisoner and slashed through them in a handful of strokes.

'You all right now?' he asked softly.

She rubbed her wrists where the ropes had chafed

into the flesh, then nodded, her features a pale blur in the darkness. For a moment she sagged against him and he felt the warmth of her body, smelled the faint perfume of her hair. Then she had straightened abruptly, drawing away from him as Everett's harsh voice yelled from outside:

'You all right, Bob?'

Cautiously Wade approached the window, taking care not to expose himself. He let the silence grow long, knew that Everett would yell again. This time the rancher called: 'Ned. Swing round the back of the shack. I reckon that Halleran has got Bob. You watch the back and I'll stay here. We can wait him out, I reckon.'

'You're wrong, Everett,' Wade called after a few moments, after he had deliberately let the silence drag once more. 'This is the end of the trail for you. Ned won't be helpin' you now. Better come forward with your hands lifted.'

'You're bluffin', Halleran. There'll be a bunch of my men ridin' up here any time now. You don't think I'd be fool enough to ride in alone, do you?'

'Sure.' Wade felt certain that the other was bluffing him. 'My guess is that you sent your men to do your dirty work for you, to attack Kerby's place.' He heard the girl give a sharp gasp behind him, but went on remorselessly. 'Somehow I hope you did. Because by now, the rest of the ranchers in the territory will have joined forces there and this time your men will find themselves to be outnumbered.'

'You're lyin',' snarled the other from the darkness. Wade tried to locate the origin of the other's voice, but he seemed to be moving around slowly and in the echoing spaces between the tumble-down buildings, the sounds kept losing themselves, becoming spread out. 'Those other men know better than to try to step up against me.'

147

'Maybe they did once, but I guess they know better now. Ever since some of your men got shot up when they tried to haze off some of the Lazy D cattle, they've got around to figurin' that maybe the Everett gunslingers can be killed like any other men if folk only have the guts to face up to them.'

The other did not reply. As the seconds dragged by into minutes, Wade stared through the glassless window, trying to probe the darkness for the other. Behind him, Jennifer said quietly, but with a faint tremor in her voice: 'Were you speaking the truth when you said that the other ranches have joined forces with my father to fight Everett's gun crew, Wade?'

He hesitated for a moment, sensed that she had drawn a little way from him, distrusting him. 'The chances are that they have,' he muttered defensively. 'But whether they have or not, I've still got to get you out of here. If I can either drop Everett or take him back with me, I figure that we'll have nothin' to fear from the men who ride with him. They're gunslingers, killers, men with the law breathin' continually down their necks. They only owe allegiance to Everett so long as he's in a position to protect them from the law. As soon as that protection ends, then their loyalty to him finishes. It's as simple as that.'

'I only wish that I could believe you,' she said dully. 'But I've known Hugh Everett for a long time. He isn't the sort of man to give in easily.'

Wade started to answer, then stopped, pulled himself to one side as a gun blasted from one of the buildings on the opposite side of the trail. He saw the muzzle flash, lacing the darkness with a streaking stiletto of flame, heard the leaden smack of the slug as it struck the wooden post near the window. Jerking up his own weapon, he fired back. The echoes died away and in the ensuing silence, he listened for movement.

When there was nothing, he called: 'You don't have a

chance, Everett. If you want to, step out on to the street and meet me face to face.'

'This is good enough for me,' came the reply. 'I never did fancy a shoot-out with a killer like you. I saw what happened to Clem.'

Wade listened to the voice very carefully this time. He placed its source somewhere along a row consisting of three shacks, swung his head a little, saw nothing. The other was almost perfectly blended with the blackness.

'Stay here,' he said to the girl, his tone more rough than he had intended. 'This is somethin' I've come a long way to finish.'

'You're not goin' out there into the street,' said the girl, a note of alarm in her voice. 'He's not to be trusted to give you an even break. He'll shoot you down from cover without a second thought.'

'I know that,' murmured Wade grimly. 'But if I don't force the issue now, he'll make a break for his horse and then we'll lose him in the darkness. Once he links up with his men we're right back where we started. The fates were on our side when he rode out here alone and it's up to me to see that they stay the same way.'

'Don't push your luck too far with Everett,' warned the girl. But she was talking to herself. Wade had already opened the door and slipped through it into the darkness, moving swiftly around the edge of the shack. He knew roughly where Hugh Everett was now. If the other did mean to make a try for his mount and ride out of this trap which he had dug for himself, then he would have to come out into the street or work his way all that distance back to where the other three horses were tethered. Somehow, he didn't think that Everett would do that. It would be too easy for him to pick him off in the saddle if he tried to ride through. No, he'd try for the horse that stood patiently in front of the shack less than twenty yards away.

He let a full minute pile up, the stillness growing in intensity until it could almost have been sliced with a knife.

'I'm coming forward Everett,' he called softly into the darkness. He moved out into the street on soft foot, making no sound. He meant to force Everett to move across to the narrow opening between two of the shacks. Once there his body would be silhouetted against the night sky, which here was a little lighter than the ground.

There was no movement from Everett. Trailing his hand along the wooden posts that had been hammered into the ground along the sides of the trail at regular intervals, he felt the worn bridle hanging there, thrust the gun into its holster and lifted the bridle down. It was tattered and broken, but he held it balanced in his hand for a moment and then threw it along the street. It struck some distance away and drew another shot from the hidden man. Even before the slug struck the dirt where the bridle had fallen, Wade's gun was in his hand again, belching flame and lead, sending two bullets at the rancher. One of them struck. He heard the other give out a heavy grunt and there was the sound of a body collapsing against one of the buildings. The other's breath quickened and drew deeper.

Wade stood still for a second, then ran forward over the trail, paused for a moment as he neared one of the alleys, moved into the darkness more slowly, the gun still clutched in his hand. He heard a faint sigh from directly in front of him and the next instant his leg struck something soft and yielding. Bending over the other, he felt for the rancher's hand. There was cold steel under his fingers and he took the gun from the other's limp grasp and tossed it away into the street. It fell with a soft thunk into the dirt.

Everett groaned softly in his throat, twisted a little, then fell back, his head striking an out-thrusting section of wood. 'You won't live to taste victory, Halleran,' he got out, voice halting at intervals. 'Elmore will—'

He stopped speaking and lay so quiet on the ground that Wade thought he was dead. Vaguely he was aware of the girl running over the trail towards him, her breathing harsh and hurried.

Everett stirred again, slowly and painfully, the effort costing him dearly. He swallowed, went on: 'Elmore will get you for this. He's—' There was a rattle in his throat, a long, drawn-out sigh that whistled through his parted teeth and then he went completely limp. Mechanically, Wade felt for the pulse in the other's wrist. It beat jerkily for a few seconds and then ceased altogether. Slowly he let the rancher's hand fall on to his chest, straightened up with a grunt, coming to his feet. He stared across the dead man's body at the girl, trying to read the look on her face. Then she said, her voice very low and soft: 'Do you think that this killing solves anything, Wade?'

'I don't know. I hope so.' He rubbed the back of his hand over his forehead, felt the sweat cold on his brow. He had thought that once he had met Everett and finished this chore, he would have felt a sense of satisfaction, of fulfilment. But curiously there was nothing like that. He had killed this man in fair fight and yet there was only a numbed emptiness in his mind.

Taking the girl's arm, he led her back to the shack, then pointed at Everett's mount. 'You'd better take that horse,' he said. 'I'll bring up mine and we'll take Everett's body back into town.'

Elmore rode at the head of fifteen men from the Everett spread shortly before sundown, their horses drumming rhythmically on the trail as they swept closer to the boundary with the Lazy D ranch. Elmore rode in grim silence, his lips pressed tightly together.

Everett's orders had been quite specific. While the other had ridden out to check on the girl, the rest of the men were to destroy Kerby and his ranch. He had only once paused to ask himself why Everett himself was not there, leading the men. The only answer he had come up with was that the other was not sure, within himself, that this time they would be successful. Those two instances when they had been shot up trying to raid the Lazy D cattle had obviously shaken his nerve a little and he did not want to be around in case anything did go wrong.

He put the idea out of his mind as it intruded again. Maybe this was correct, but even so, he had a chore to do and the hell with fooling around! They reached the boundary fence and he sat tall and still in the saddle, as three of the man lassoed the posts, tore them from the ground. Trampling the wire into the dirt, they rode over it, across the flat pasture land, making good time with the sun just touching the flat horizon by the time they topped a low rise and saw the lights of the Lazy D ranch directly ahead of them, nestling in the small hollow. He reined up his mount directly on top of the rise, sat forward a little in the saddle, his arms resting on the pommel. He scanned the outbuildings closely, saw no movement. There was, he noticed, a plume of grey smoke issuing from the chimney, but apart from that and the horses in the circular corral, there were no other signs of life.

Too quiet, murmured a little warning thought at the back of his mind. Too goddamned quiet. It had that feel about it which he had sensed at other times in the past shortly before all hell erupted, breaking loose around him. Lowering his right hand, he loosened the Colt in its holster, working the weapon up and down a little.

One of the men, edging his horse forward, said softly 'Seems to be a lot of horses in that corral, Elmore.'

The big foreman gave a brusque nod. 'So I'd noticed,'

he said shortly. 'You thinkin' the same as I am?'

'That they may have got help from some of the other ranchers?'

'That's right. It's beginnin' to look that way to me. They must be fools though to let the horses stand out there in the corral warnin' us.'

The other man was silent for a long moment, then he said thoughtfully: 'Unless they got only a handful of men and they put out those critters to fool us.'

Elmore pondered that for a long moment, then said through thinly-stretched lips. 'Could be. Either way, we'll take 'em without too much trouble. Swing round and come in from all sides. We'll cut 'em to ribbons in a crossfire.'

Swiftly conceived on the spur of the moment, the plan was just as swiftly put into operation. The men spread out swiftly, put their horses down the slope, riding hard at the ranch. They were three hundred yards from it and still no sign of life. Two hundred and there was a wolfish grin on Elmore's face. This was going to be too easy, he thought exultantly.

Then pandemonium broke loose. His earlier thought that it might be a trap proved to be only too correct. Rifle and pistol fire broke out from every window in the ranch house and from the bunkhouse too, lead singing through the darkening gloom. Three of the Everett riders were cut from their saddles in as many seconds, pitching sideways and rolling drunkenly over the smooth ground. The rest reined up their mounts. Too much like suicide to ride on into that blistering, withering hail of murderous fire.

Dropping to the ground they scattered for cover. Another rider fell before he gained sanctuary. Elmore sank down on to his knees in a small hollow, drew a bead on a vague shape that showed momentarily at one of the windows, fired without seeming to take conscious aim. The shape vanished and Elmore pressed off another shot as a man ran from the bunkhouse, heading towards the ranch. The shape staggered, lurched, pulled itself together and ran on for a couple of faltering steps before collapsing in a heap in the middle of the courtyard.

Grinning wolfishly, Elmore yelled: 'Bart, Williams and Thomas, round to the rear of the place. The rest of you move in. Those with rifles lay a barrage on the front of the ranch. You can make matchwood out of it.'

The men trotted off into the gloom, sliding down through the wet grass on the slope of the hill, pausing whenever slugs whined near them from the Lazy D men. Elmore studied the terrain. Two of his men ran forward towards the long, low horse trough near the edge of the corral. A hail of fire from inside the bunkhouse met them, slewing them sideways, driving both men several paces over the dirt before they dropped dead against the wooden fence. At the same instant, more firing broke out in the distance.

'The others must've tangled with them at the back,' said the man lying on his belly close to the foreman.

Elmore reloaded his weapon, looked over the sights for a target. Most of the Lazy D men were keeping down out of sight, showing themselves only for brief instants whenever they fired. Elmore could see dust kicking up around those of his men closest to the house. He knew now that by some means, Kerby had got more men from somewhere to back his play. For the first time he could see ultimate victory slipping from his grasp. He gritted his teeth, yelled to the men to lay down covering fire, ordering others to rush forward.

'Get some torches and we'll burn 'em out,' he shouted at the top of his lungs.

Three men moved off from the lower slopes, up to the brush on top of the hill. They returned a few minutes later with the rapidly improvised torches, lit them and held them aloft as they prepared to run forward under the withering fire from the men with rifles along the lower slope.

'Soon as we all open up, get movin',' he said tightly. 'Once we get a few torches in there the whole place will go up like tinder.'

Again the continual smash of shots ripped the twilight apart. Elmore and the men near him loosed off a rapid succession of shots against the ranch house. Chips of wood flew from the posts along the front of the building. Then the men with the torches began to move in, bending low to present more difficult targets. But to Elmore's consternation it was soon painfully obvious that the Lazy D men had outguessed them again, had seen the danger and were ready for it. One man fell forward as bullets smashed into his back. Another reeled drunkenly, striving to keep a grip on the blazing torch. The third man took half a dozen slow and faltering steps, then began to weave erratically across the courtyard, the torch falling from his fingers before another volley cut him down.

A voice from the ranch which Elmore recognized a second later as Kerby's, called savagely: 'If you're out there Everett, come on in – were're just beginnin' to get warmed up here. This is where we finish you for good.'

Elmore, in spite of himself, felt a little chill of apprehension go through him. A little tremor in his legs began to work its way up into his body. The possibility of defeat had not entered his mind until this very moment, but it did now. A steady storm of lead poured into the men crouched down at the bottom of the hill, keeping them pinned down, unable to move backward or forward.

Elmore sucked in a deep breath. Inwardly, he still felt that savage, bitter lust to kill, a primeval urge to destroy. But without men to back his play he realized that it was impossible to go on. He seemed to have deliberately led these men into a trap and his mind spun in a tight web as he tried to find a way out of it. This was something he had not bargained for. How had Kerby managed to talk these yellow-livered ranchers into helping him? And where in hell's name was Everett? This was his show, no one else's when it came to the point. Why was he not here, risking his life with the others?

More slugs hummed through the air, smashing into the earth near his prone body, ricocheting with thin, high-pitched shrieks of tortured metal off the rocks. A blue laze of gunsmoke hung unmoving in the still air. Gasping and weaving, he got to his feet, moved back a short distance, threw himself down behind a clump of mesquite as the accurate fire followed him. It seemed incredible that they could have spotted his movement in the growing darkness.

'We don't stand a chance now,' said the man near him, turning his head, his face grey. 'They've dropped most of the boys and we don't seem to have stopped any of them. We're too much in the open here.'

Elmore cocked his head on one side, muttered sharply: 'Keep firin'. We've still got the place surrounded. They only have a limited amount of ammunition. We'll soon wear 'em down.'

'You don't really believe that, Elmore,' said the other, his voice rising sharply in pitch as he spoke. 'I'm gettin' out of here. This is too rich for my blood. Besides, I notice that Everett ain't here to take any of the risks. He's ridden off and we won't see hair nor hide of him until it's all over, one way or the other.'

Before he had finished speaking the other had clambered clumsily to his feet. He threw a quick glance in the direction of the Lazy D ranch, saw the bright spurts of flame from the windows and turned to run, feet slipping on the wet, treacherous grass. Elmore's lips curled in a faint sneer. The other had only gone a dozen paces when a bullet cut him down. He lay moan-

ing softly on the grass for several seconds, then jerked
as a second slug found its mark in his body, rolled on to
his side and lay very still. The concentration of gunfire
from the ranch and bunkhouse was tremendous now,
smashing against the hillside.

Elmore waited for three long minutes, listening to
the terrible sound of the return fire. Nothing in his
past experience had been anything like this. He lay flat
for a while, not so much frightened as cowed by the
smashing impact of slugs all about him. Every single
muscle in him was drawn so tight that it hurt with a
physical pain that was like nothing he had ever
known. His mind felt very clear and sharp and he
knew he had to get out of there, and quickly, if he
wanted to stay alive.

He followed the shifting concentration of gunfire
with his ears and now he thought only of his own
survival. The horses were tethered near the top of the
hill and keeping his head very low, he began to crawl
towards them. The main weight of fire seemed to have
shifted to the rear of the ranch where the rest of the
men were still keeping up their futile assault. He knew
inwardly that it was now only a matter of time before
they were wiped out or forced to try to extricate themselves. Gently he eased himself out into a bare, open
patch of ground, held his breath as he wormed his way
across it. Nothing happened and he began to breathe
more easily as he got to the other side, moved towards
the horses. There was still intense firing going on
below, a racket that filled the night with a tremendous
din; and perhaps it was because of this that he had not
heard the horses approach, was not aware that there
was anyone standing there until a voice from the shadows softly called his hand.

'Stand right there, Elmore. I reckon there's a score
to settle with you.'

He tensed, made no move to go for his gun, feeling

around with his senses. Turning his head very slowly, he saw the figure that stood a short distance away, said with his lip curling derisively: 'So it is you, Halleran. I figured you might come ridin' back some time.'

'Then I reckon you know that if I did, Everett would be dead.' Without taking his glance off the foreman, Wade jerked a thumb behind him. 'That's his body across the horse yonder. Now it's your turn. Before he died Everett said that you'd get me. Well, here I am. Let's see if his confidence was badly misplaced or not.'

'Just what do you hope to get out of this, Halleran?' asked the other. His tone was flat, lacking natural curiosity. He seemed, to Wade, to be stalling for time. Somehow this did not fit in with the character of this gunslick as Wade had been told about him. 'You had a quarrel with Everett. He's dead. That ought to be it. Why throw your life away by callin' me out?'

'Because you're a two-bit killer who doesn't deserve to go on livin'.' Wade said tightly. 'Everett only hired you for one thing. To supervise his dirty work for him, see that anyone who got in his way died.'

'And you figure you can draw against me and come out on top?' There was a sneer in the killer's tone. He shook his head very slowly. There was a cruel smile on his lips.

'Seems to me that you're doin' a lot of talkin' for a man who reckons he's confident,' Wade opined. He held his hand just above the handle of the gun in its holster, fingers curved a little, his eyes not once moving from the other's gunhand. He guessed that Elmore was not nervous, that he was trying one of the oldest tricks in the book, talking in an attempt to draw his attention away from what he was going to do. A feint to give the killer the edge on the draw.

Another second went by; and all of eternity seemed to have been crowded into it. Then, jerking himself around sharply, Elmore went for his gun. It was a fast, smooth draw, almost too quick for the eye to follow. The gun jerked into his fist, cleared leather and the barrel was just beginning to bear when the blue-crimson flash, stabbing through the darkness in front of him, told him he had lost. He felt the driving, leaden impact of the slug as it struck him in the chest. His own pistol exploded as he staggered, and the slug tore into the dirt at his feet. Desperately, striving to hold life in his body for a few more seconds, he struggled to lift the gun in his hand, sobbing with rage and pain. Then his knees bent as though no longer able to hold his weight and he slid to the ground to stretch his full length on the dirt.

Wade crossed to him and knelt. Elmore gave a faint little gasp, then his head rolled on one side and all life went from him. Down below, in the valley, only an occasional shot now burned through the night. Wade went back along the trail a little way came to where the girl stood in the shadow of the tall trees. She was peering anxiously into the darkness, trying to see who it was. When she recognized him she ran forward with a faint cry, caught his arm.

'Are you all right?'

He nodded, led the way down the hillside towards the ranch. 'I'm all right,' he said quietly. 'But I think this is the end for Everett and his bunch of gun-crazy killers. Those who are still alive will be rounded up and taken into town for trial. Somehow I think that Bender's Edge will make certain that nothing like this occurs again.'

'Those are my thoughts too, Wade,' she said, equally softly. 'This is still the frontier, but it won't always be like this. Things have to change for the better.'

He nodded, stared up for a moment at the star-hung night above them, then fell into step beside her as they made their way down to the quiet ranch.